happily
murdered....

happily
murdered....

Rasleen Syal

Srishti
PUBLISHERS & DISTRIBUTORS

SRISHTI PUBLISHERS & DISTRIBUTORS
N-16, C. R. Park
New Delhi 110 019
editorial@srishtipublishers.com

First published by
Srishti Publishers & Distributors in 2014

Typeset by Eshu Graphic

To my loving parents.
Mama, for all your sacrifices over the years.
Papa, for your unconditional love and devotion.
I love you.

Acknowledgements

I owe everything I have, everything I am, to my SAI, my salvation.

My journey of writing a book started much before I actually put pen to paper. It started when I was just a little babe, as my Grandmother would have said. I still have fond memories of her reading me fairy tales every night. Over the years, I shared her love for the works of authors like Earl Stanley Gardner, Agatha Christie and Barbara Cartland. I must thank her for introducing me to the world of stories.

I have always been a rebel and the penchant to do what I am told against is in my nature. My parents often encouraged me to devote more time to my school curriculum than pleasure reading. Both being self achievers and rising up the ladder because of education and hard work had their own ideas and beliefs. Sneaking books home and reading in the light of a night bulb had a charm of its own. Though I was often caught and punished. Inadvertently my parents fanned my desire to read more and more. They have my heartfelt gratitude for all their patience with a rebellious teen.

My sister, my partner in crime, must be thanked for keeping my dates with my books a secret. She even shared her pocket money with me for renting them. Thanks for always being there.

It was my love for reading which later on morphed into writing. Writing is a lonely affair but a few people deserve to be credited for making it easier on me.

I must thank my husband for not laughing his head off when I declared my desire to write a book. He supported me in every way he could. Though he still hasn't read my work.

Shabnum, my dearest friend, my first reader, must be commended for taking a day off work to read my manuscript and give her feedback.

I owe a lot to my publisher for believing in my writing and giving me a chance to be a part of the wonderful Srishti team. He has my sincere gratitude for always being so gracious and helpful.

It was great working with Pinaki da, who not only designed a beautiful cover for the book but also gave a debut author his valuable inputs about the world of publishing.

I also must be grateful for my lucky mascot, my daughter. I signed my book deal within a week of her birth. Love you, darling.

Finally, my utmost respect to my biggest inspiration, my Guru, Agatha Christie. It is only by reading her works that I have learned to write mysteries. Agatha Christie, I am forever indebted for stimulating my little grey cells.

Prologue

People exhibit their happiness in so many ways. Cricketers so often fall down on their knees and yell out their exuberance after winning an important match, the slight tremor in an Oscar winning actor's voice while giving an acceptance speech is proof enough of his feelings, proud parents express it with tight hugs and a sweetheart kisses with a passionate abandon to communicate what words can't.

She was dancing.

Her henna clad feet were moving in quick rotating circles on the cold marble floor. Dressed in her wedding finery, she was clutching her *duppata* which was moving as one with her body, one edge in her hand and the other touching the periphery with its flow. Chin held high, long jet black hair clasping her body with her circular movements and her *lehenga* swish swashing around her legs, she radiated elation. There was no trace of make up on her face, her body bare of any kind of jewellery except a star shaped shimmering pendant clasped around her neck on a thin silver chain. Sheer joy and contentment drugged her into closing her eyes, helping a tear escape. It glistened down her smooth cheek and settled in the vicinity of a soft smile.

She did not know for how long she had been gliding with the cool breeze. Neither did she want to. She just wanted this day to never end. Her legs started to give way but she continued to move with the same rhythm, willing herself to prolong this pleasure for as long as possible. The circles became irregular; she collided with something or someone. She did not care or open her eyes. It slowed her down but she gained her pace again. Exhaustion was setting in and her movements seemed to lose momentum, just like her favourite ride, the merry-go-round towards the end. She realized the truth of her own merry-go-round and submitted to the rule of its stopping at the end of an exhilarating ride.

Her graceful body succumbed to the promise of rest after a tiring albeit satisfying journey. Her limbs gave way and with a thud she fell on the cold floor. She embraced it with the warmth of love emanating from her. Lying on her back, she gazed fondly at the twinkling stars crooning softly to her from their perch on the beds of clouds. The silver stars looked rosy to her, peering at them as she was, from under her red netted dupatta.

Taking a deep breath she closed her eyes capturing the vision of the effervescent night before it hid behind the twilight's curtain which she knew would soon turn into dawn.

A few minutes later, lying there in the tantalizing night she seemed perfectly serene.

The day was everything Gulab had always wanted. And this was the perfect end.

My End is My Beginning

I could see the most beautiful backyard I had ever seen from up here. It seemed like a flower strewn colourful meadow with a small lake a little way down the slope. Right in the middle of it a pavilion rested on stone buttresses, famously known as The Dancing Pavilion. Around twenty feet in diameter, it had a wooden balustrade and was covered with a canopy supported by pillars.

The sun had just started to throw around faint rays of light on the horizon. The chirping of the birds drew my attention towards the meadows. I was delighted by the autumn foliage as always. The colour of the autumn leaves mystify me. How does a maple leaf turn bright red? Where did all the yellows and oranges come from?

Autumn indeed is my favourite season.

My feet crunched the dried leaves covering the ground as I moved towards my favourite spot; the lake. Yet, neither the tranquil waters of the lake delicately caressing the foot of the pavilion nor the tall Sal tree encircled in the protective embrace of the colourful hills could hold my interest for long.

Today she held my attention completely, lying on her back in the middle of the Pavilion dressed in her wedding lehenga choli.

I started gravitating towards her taking the wooden bridge connecting the pavement to the pavilion. The air was chilly and I wrapped my dupatta *around my shoulders. It was the softest net*

1

fabric, embroidered at the hems with corals and silken threads, but was no protection for the early autumn mornings in the hills. Reaching the pavilion, I touched the balustrade and moved around its circumference feeling the cold surface under my palms. The scent wafting from the flowers had sweetened the air and I took big gulps into my lungs. It was mingled with her perfume. Its sublime floral melody with a romantic trail between dream and reality enticed me towards her. I could identify the Ninna Ricci fragrance; Love in Paris. I had been using the same for ages.

I could no longer avoid looking at her. I stole a quick glance in her direction and was astounded by the beauty of the picture I saw. I bent my knees and crouched near her. Her lips had an innocent smile floating on them. Somehow she seemed fairer than usual today, her net dupatta covering half of her face. My henna clad hand touched her white cheek delicately. I half expected her to open her eyes and chide me for disturbing her flight of dreams. But she remained serene; smiling at the world her dreams had conjured up for her.

I have never seen a corpse look so ethereal. Somehow she didn't seem without life. Anyone who knew her could easily say that she emanated far too much verve today, more than she had done in her entire life. Anyway, who knew her more than me? I drew my net dupatta tighter around me and brushed the lonely tear glistening on my cheek near my lip. It had been resting there since my dance of passion last night.

It was difficult to believe that this girl, this haunting beauty, used to be me.

A Cortege of Mourners - 1

I

"Do you also think that Sara did it?"

The appeal in the young man's voice and pain in his eyes touched the old lady's heart. Her wrinkled hand patted his sinewy arm sympathetically.

Removing her gold rimmed glasses she let them dangle from the thick gold chain around her neck and scrunching her withered grey eyes peered closely at him. After a minute of thoughtful consideration, she spoke in a voice too tired to hurry but too powerful to slow down. Old age had taken a toll on her body but not her spirit.

"Ned dear, I know she could never do it," she stressed, "even if she tried. She doesn't have a mean bone in her body."

Mrs. Sarojini Mehta, called Biji by family, was an eighty-six year old lady with a masterful cast of features and indomitable spirit. Rheumatism had rendered her unable to walk but she did not let that deter her from enjoying the pace of her life. She had aligned herself so closely with her wheel chair that it had become an extended body part of hers. Her husband had been a famous hotelier of Punjab. Widowed at the age of thirty, she had singlehandedly managed her husband's business and taken care of her three-year-old son. Under her wing the business had flourished exponentially and she was considered a path breaker in the Indian hospitality industry. Twenty years ago she had handed down the reins of the business completely to her son, KD, and retired.

While on a sojourn to look over a property, to convert it into a heritage hotel, Mrs. Mehta had visited Ratnagiri forty years ago. She had instantly fallen in love with this small town located in the tranquil Himalayan foothills, close to the mythological cities of Haridwar and Rishikesh, surrounded by graceful Sal forests and overlooking the peaceful Ganga as it meandered into the distance.

Ratnagiri lies nestled on the southern slopes of the Shivalik hills in the Gadhwal Region. Now a small constituency forming a part of the state of Uttaranchal, it was once a princely state ruled by the Dulla family, with Ratnagiri as its summer capital and the Palace as the official residence. The changing face of post-freedom India, soon wiped out princely roles and the family sold the property and turned to politics in order to survive.

While negotiating the deal with the Dullas, Mrs. Mehta befriended the royal family. The Dulla family constituted of the Maharaja, his wife, an elder daughter and two sons. The daughter was married and settled in London. After selling off the estate, the Maharaja migrated to Delhi along with his younger son. The elder Dulla son and heir to the throne, Dilip Dulla, moved in with his sister in London to complete his studies. He went on to become a famed travel writer. He married a British heiress and frequently visited India to do research for his books. His family often holidayed in Ratnagiri where they had an ancestral farm house and the friendship between the two families remained strong over the years.

And it was this friendship which made Biji commit, "Don't worry, child. We will fight tooth and nail for Sara. The whole Mehta family is with you."

Biji looked appreciatively at Ned Dulla and thought how like his twin he looked. Both had auburn hair and light eyes. A slender build, delicate features and a prominent straight nose coupled with a pale complexion gave away his origins. He was the replica of his British mother.

"How did this all happen?!" It wasn't a question but a sigh of despondency from Ned.

"It is all that girl, Gulab's, doing. What family values did she have with both parents divorced and remarried?" Biji was of the old school of thought and her moral policing had reared its head and found Gulab wanting as her grandson's future wife. "Rich but no class!" She added snobbishly.

Ned didn't agree with Biji's harsh opinion, after all Gulab didn't get murdered on purpose, he sighed. But he knew better than to refute Biji just now. Biji was in an unusually pleasant mood, Ned thought, considering not even a week had passed since Gulab and Sid's marriage and Gulab's death. Everyone in Ratnagiri Palace was dismal but not Biji. He had come to visit her after his sister's arrest and subsequent bail in Gulab's murder case. According to the police, Sara was the prime suspect but Biji had rubbished it and her army of lawyers had marched forth and within hours of her arrest had got her release orders. Ned *was* grateful.

"Now, Sara, on the other hand," Biji smiled, "She is all class. I have been observing her for years. Her dignified bearing and gentle nature has always pulled at my heart strings."

She continued after a small pause.

"It was my wish to welcome her into our family as Siddharth's wife," she sighed regretfully.

Until a few months ago Biji had been very close to getting her wish fulfilled but she had smouldered in silent rage when Sid broke up his engagement with Sara and decided to get married to Gulab instead.

Shaking the gloom off, she looked hopefully at Ned, "With Gulab dead, maybe we still have hope."

Ned nodded, though he didn't agree with her.

She said consolingly to him:

"Dear, you go home to Sara and rest assured that all of us are with you."

"Thank you, Biji." Ned got up, a suggestion of deference in his manner, and took his leave.

She smiled fondly at the retreating figure.

Putting her glasses back on and adjusting the blue and pink *phulkari* dupatta over her pink *salwaar suit*, Biji wheeled her chair towards the French windows. Those who knew her well could easily tell her mood by the colours she sported. She had this weird habit of dressing up according to her disposition and pink symbolized that she was perky and happy today. Reaching up she pulled the curtains aside. Sunlight flowed in the room and drenched her old wrinkled body with warmth. Her silver hair tied at the back of her head in a severe knot gleamed more than ever. She positioned her spectacles on the bridge of her hooked nose. Shading her eyes from the sun she looked out towards the lake and the Dancing Pavilion. Out of the corner of her eye she thought she saw a shadow walk down the bridge. A tremor shook her hand covered with age spots and she closed her faded grey eyes for a minute before opening them to look into the distance once more. There was no one in the backyard. She sighed with satisfaction and relaxed in her chair, at peace with the outcome of Sid's marriage.

II

The unmistakable sound of her son's Harley Davidson forced Mrs. Tina Mehta out of her reverie. She had been totally absorbed in appraising the facts of Gulab's death. Tina was disappointed by her death. She was a social butterfly and had made great plans of broadening her social circle using Gulab's contacts. Her father was a prominent member of the ruling party of the state and owing to the Mehtas' connection with the Dullas, who were aligned with one of the smaller opposition parties, the Mehtas were not close to the most prominent and powerful politicians of the state. But all that could have been remedied by Gulab's presence in the Mehtas' circle. Tina fancied herself in the role of a political activist with the ruling party of the state, undefeated for the last thirty years, and fate had presented a shortcut to her. But after Gulab's death things couldn't progress as she had planned, she sighed sadly.

Tina was the only daughter of a wealthy Hotelier from New York. At the age of twenty-two she had married the successful and debonair Mr. Karan Deep Mehta who was six years older than her. The marriage was arranged by KD's autocratic mother. KD and Tina had been happily married for the last thirty five years, pursuing their own passions, making money and spending money respectively.

Tina could hear her youngest son, Yuvi's, bike roaring on the property and the crude noise worsened her already strained mood. She was reclining on an elegant antique settee in the living room. Its thirty feet high dome looked magnificently huge and the curving staircase winding towards the upper storey added to its majestic look. The furniture was Victorian in style. The floor was covered with a Persian hand-woven carpet in rich colours. The Mehta family had not only helped retain the air of royalty for the Palace but had added many folds to its charms by the strategic use of money and good taste.

Tina left her comfortable perch and moved towards the French windows which opened onto the porch. She was not a pessimist and her mood lifted instantly when she realized that at her son's lavish wedding she had made quite a few contacts. She could take things forward from there. Also Gulab's mysterious death opened a number of gates for her. She realized people were always interested in gossip, what a good topic for conversation it would be, all the gory details that too from one of the family. She expected quite a stir around her after a suitable period of mourning. Her spirits revived, she went out to greet her son and his irksome bike.

III

A ride on his Harley Davidson never failed to drive all thoughts away from Yuvraj's mind.

The wind ruffled his close cropped hair, as dark as the night sky. His stubbled face reverberated with rugged masculinity and the silver ear-ring in his pierced ear added to his rakish looks. These last few days, for him, had rippled with emotions he was too weak to accept. So, yes, his Harley was helping him deal with the situation. He rode and rode and rode and then rode some more in order to dodge reality.

He closed his eyes for a second to suppress Gulab's memories and increased the speed of his bike.

Ratnagiri has narrow roads like all small hilly towns but this did not deter Yuvi from pushing his Harley to its limits. After all, his own property accorded him quite a few advantages. The Ratnagiri Palace is on the cliff of a hill. This property is locally known as The Royal Hill. The Palace grounds cover twenty-six acres, out of which the constructed area covers three and a half acres while fifteen acres are devoted to the gardens. The entrance is guarded by huge white gates and running along the periphery of the property is a ten feet high wall. It secludes the Royal Hill from the trespassers. The main gate is connected to the Palace building with a three kilometre long winding driveway adding charm to the colourful front gardens. And this snakelike meandering path was where Yuvi's bike vented its venom.

Tina watched him drive down the path. His tall dark frame made him look attractive; Tina nodded appreciatively. But like most of the people who knew her three sons, Sid was always considered the best looking of them all. Yuvi was more muscular and taller than Sid. Both were handsome in their own ways, Sid being an Apollo and Yuvi a Hercules. Sid's easy manner and a ready smile made him very popular. Yuvi's aloofness on the other hand made him seem unapproachable. He had a short, dry and caustic manner which had made his mother nickname him the 'angry young man' of the family.

Much to the chagrin of their mother, her eldest son Vikram didn't make it to the list of the desirable men in the town. A jolly bumbling man, more often than not immersed in work like his father, he wasn't, however, as business savvy as the latter. He didn't have much time for friends; his wife being his only confidante. In her hands he was putty, she wielded a power over him like no one else could, Tina scoffed.

Yuvi parked his bike on the porch and alighted from his perch. Dressed as usual in ripped jeans and a t-shirt, he was in the process of removing his aviators but seeing his mother waiting for him he let them be. They shielded his eyes from the harsh sun but more importantly from the onlookers. His eyes never lied and he didn't want anyone to peep into his turbulent heart.

"I don't like the noise you make with that bike of yours. It disturbs us all, Yuvi," his mother reprimanded him as soon as he entered the living room.

"This noise is not good for me. I hear it and frown," she gingerly touched her forehead, feeling around for any frown lines. "You know I am not young anymore and frown lines can etch permanently on my forehead," she sighed worriedly. "Why do you ride that monster on the property unnecessarily?" Her voice was exasperated.

Yuvi hugged his belligerent mother and replied in his characteristic, short and terse manner.

"Didn't think you would be up. Not noon yet." He lounged back on the sofa, jeans stretching on his strong thighs and continued, "Whatever your age, you'll always look beautiful," he smiled curtly, inwardly thinking about the Botox treatments his mother had got.

He was right though. Tina Mehta could battle any frown lines daring to surface on her smooth skin, adroitly. She was fifty-six, but had one of those smooth ageless faces that change little with passing years. She had a slight frame and a striking profile with a slender bridged nose. She styled her hair in chic hairdos, changing them every few weeks and was sporting a wavy bob these days. She had a penchant for getting hair treatments, experimenting with different colours, extensions, curls, rebonding or highlights.

"It has been a hell of a time, these last few days. It's no surprise that I am sitting idle in the living room in the middle of the morning," Tina cribbed.

"I know," Yuvi sighed and his face softened realizing that even his hard boiled mother was sorry for their loss. "Gulab's death has upset us all," his Adam's apple bobbled with emotion. "Don't think too much about it," he advised.

His mother looked at him as if he had lost his mind and replied in her frank manner, "I am not thinking too much about Gulab or her murder. Dear God! I am not a detective. What has happened has happened. For the last ten days I have been sitting here doing nothing, no party invitations and convention forbids me to go out and have a good time. I slept at ten! Me! That's why I have had my coffee by eleven in the morning. The only excursion I have had is a visit to the spa. I had to get the fiery red highlights I was sporting for the marriage off my hair," she combed a hand through her short loose strands, "the colour was just not becoming me. But I had to wait for a whole week before I could visit the spa. And I even had to cancel my other regular appointments!"

Her delicate manicured hands were drawn out as if asking for understanding for her sorry plight, "That stupid girl had to go out and die so near the fashion week. I would have been having the time of my life if she hadn't messed it up!" she grumbled.

Shaking her head at Gulab's foolishness she marched towards the bar to concoct a cocktail. Yuvi looked at her and a keen observer may have surprised a tear rolling from under his sunglasses.

He got up and started to climb the stairs two at a time leaving his callous mother to get drunk before the afternoon sun even reared its head.

As he was crossing the landing he thought that he saw a reflection in the glass of a picture on the wall. He looked around him but there was no one on the stairs. He walked towards the picture, his expression morphing into disgust; nose flaring with anger and eyes filling with contempt. It was a childhood photo of him and Sid. He couldn't stop himself from tearing it away from the wall, throwing it on the floor and crushing it mercilessly with his feet.

IV

Modern technologies had made life much simpler and yet so complex. Vikram rubbed his eyes tiredly. He was working on his laptop, trying to compile all communications from Gulab; mails, chats, and offliners. He had diligently saved them all for he always tried to imitate his father's style of doing business; methodical, everything written, signed and documented. He chastised himself inwardly for not cataloguing everything like his father recommended. Tallying the financials without Gulab's help was becoming too cumbersome for him.

Vikram was a big man, pot bellied and jovial. Small round eyes, a snub nose, pink puckered lips and a peachy complexion gave him a childlike appearance. Even his receding hairline couldn't distract from his green image and his bumbling manner helped reinforce it every now and then. He tried to copy Sid's crisp dressing sense but trying too hard to be stylish was his undoing. His appearance completely masked his true nature for what hid behind his merry and slightly foolish manner was pure malice. He fed on jealousy, insecurity and competition.

A compulsive eater, Vikram took out a bar of chocolate from a drawer and munched on it for a minute before getting back to his work.

His thoughts drifted to the time he had thought his dreams were so very close to his grasp. Vikram's dream project had needed investment and Gulab had agreed to finance it. He had gladly offered partnership in return. The Indian ministry of tourism had identified thirty-one villages across the country to be developed as tourist hubs and Vikram had managed to get the tender for Himachal Pradesh. The Mehta Group's experience in real estate development in the tourism sector and Gulab's political clout had helped them cut through the competition.

He had been working with his father for the last twelve years. Everyone knew him as KD Mehta's big bumbling son and he was deeply perturbed by this. Vikram desperately wanted to establish his own identity. His inherent insecurity was fanned by his father's cosseting attitude and his wife's constant reminders that Sid was the more favoured son, which was true to a certain extent. This venture meant doing something for once without his father overshadowing him.

KD Mehta did not approve of his decision to go solo on this project but Vikram didn't heed his advice. Vikram had wanted to cut off his ties from the family business but KD dashed his desires arguing about the tainted image of the Mehta Group which would be the inevitable result in case of a split in the family. However, Vikram had been adamant, and so, KD proposed a mutually beneficial solution. The project would ensue as a joint venture between The Mehta Group and Gulab's company for the first quarter and then Gulab could take over the project with Vikram having stake in her company.

The Mehtas would make up some valid excuse in the meantime citing that Vikram being close to the project would want to carry on with Gulab's company.

If truth be told, KD didn't want his eldest son to venture out alone and jeopardize the family solidarity. He hated any kind of subterfuge to his authority as well. In KD's eyes the motto of the Mehta clan was to stay united and he was the front runner for the cause.

In these last three months, KD had tried every trick of the trade to make Gulab back out of the arrangement but his constant persecution couldn't change her mind in the least. This not only soured the relationship between father and son but also drove a wedge between Gulab and KD.

Vikram was delighted to have Gulab as his partner, at least in the beginning. But what he hadn't bargained for was Gulab's continuous interference. She was extremely intelligent and astute. Her perception and logical approach saved them quite a few times but made the maladroit Vikram look like an idiot in front of his own employees and board. He could see another KD of the future in Gulab. Vikram started resenting her presence and continuously found ways to alienate her from the business.

Little did he know how things would change if she was not around. But how could he have known about Gulab's will? Had he only known, he sighed for the umpteenth time.

With Gulab gone, her assets now her husband Sid's, Vikram was at sea about the future of his venture. He could ask Sid for help but knowing him as well as he did, Vikram was sure that Sid wouldn't go against their father. Also, he knew something else which no one else did. Vikram had been saving this information to use against Sid at the right time but with Gulab's demise it didn't hold value anymore. Sid was deep in debt, a side-effect of his affection with horse racing and affliction with the loan sharks. With Gulab's money Sid's problems would now be a hardship of the past, never reaching his father's ears.

He wolfed down the whole bar of chocolate before banging shut his laptop.

He closed his eyes and mouthed mournfully, "Why didn't I consider the consequences of my actions? Why?"

Gulab Sarin Murder Case Report

Reporting Official's Name - Sub Inspector Pankaj Sharma

Case - 32C15A

Murder of Ms. Gulab Sarin

Ratnagiri Police Station

Case in charge – ASP Indra Naik

Police Surgeon and Forensic Head - Dr. Amar Malik

Case Facts

Date of crime – 8 August, 20--

Body discovered by – Ms. Upma (Maid)

Time of discovering body – 5:30am

Forensic Report for the Victim

Cause of death – Potassium Cyanide Poisoning.

Time of death – Between 2:00am and 4:00am.

Declared items on victim's body – None (Only clothes).

Case Summary

The victim and her husband reached Ratnagiri Palace after their marriage ceremony, at 11:00 pm. The puja rituals were conducted till 12:30 am. The victim was seen alive by multiple witnesses till that time. All members of the household were present in the ritual.

The maid discovered the body on the pavilion in the morning and woke the family up. The body was touched by various family members as murder was not suspected at once. Dr. A Rajnish was called and he suspected foul play and called the police.

The police reached the spot at 6:45am. The regular procedure of investigation was conducted. Following is the gist of statements given by the people present in the Palace on the day of crime.

1. Mrs. Sarojini Mehta

- Relation to the victim – Grandmother-in-law.
- Age – 86 years.
- Last saw the victim alive at 12:30 am.
- Went to bed at 12:45 am.
- Activity report between 12:30 am and 12:45 am – getting ready for bed.
- Activity report between 2:00 am and 4:00 am – sleeping.
- Alibi – none.
- Any Motive for wanting victim dead – no.
- Rapport with victim – had known victim since she was a child. Believed to be fond of her.

2. Mr. K D Mehta

- Relation to the victim – Father-in-law.
- Age – 62 years.
- Last saw the victim alive at 12:30 am.

- Went to bed at 1:00 am.
- Activity report between 12:30 am and 1:00 am – getting ready for bed.
- Activity report between 2:00 am and 4:00 am – sleeping.
- Alibi – none.
- Any motive for wanting victim dead – no.
- Rapport with victim – had known victim since she was a child. Was happy with the marriage of his son with the victim because of the financial and political standing of victim's family.

3. Mrs. Tina Mehta

- Relation to the victim – Mother-in-law.
- Age – 56 years.
- Last saw the victim alive at 12:30 am.
- Went to bed at 1:30 am.
- Activity report between 12:30 am and 1:30 am – getting ready for bed.
- Activity report between 2:00 am and 4:00 am – sleeping.
- Alibi – no.
- Any motive for wanting victim dead – no.
- Rapport with victim – had known victim since she was a child. Had liked her as a person and was happy with the marriage of her son with the victim.

4. Mr. Vikram Mehta

- Relation to the victim – Brother-in-law and Business partner.
- Age – 35 years.

- Last saw the victim alive at 1:00 am.
- Went to bed at 1:30 am.
- Activity report between 12:30 am and 1:30 am – was with the bride and groom till 1:00 am. Went to his room after that.
- Activity report between 2:00 am and 4:00 am – sleeping.
- Alibi –none.
- Any motive for wanting victim dead – no.
- Rapport with victim – good.

5. Mrs. Monica Mehta
- Relation to the victim – Sister-in-law.
- Age – 32 years.
- Last saw the Victim Alive at 1:00 am.
- Went to bed at 1:30 am.
- Activity report between 12:30 am and 1:30 am – Was with the bride and groom till 1:00 am. Went to her room after that and got ready for bed.
- Activity report between 2:00 am and 4:00 am – sleeping.
- Alibi – none.
- Any Motive for wanting victim dead – yes.
- (a) Her younger sister was engaged to Siddharth Mehta four months ago. The engagement was broken and Siddharth got involved with the victim. She may have been bitter about this.
- (b) Her younger brother was in a relationship with the victim before she got engaged to Siddharth Mehta and broke off with him for the same reason. She may have been bitter about this.
- Rapport with victim – Did not like the victim much.

Was civil to her but didn't appreciate the marriage.

6. Mr. Siddharth Mehta

- Relation to the victim – Husband.
- Age – 28 years.
- Last saw the victim Alive at 2:00 am (approximate).
- Went to bed at 2:00 am (approximate).
- Activity report between 12:30 am and 2:00 am – Was with his brothers, sister-in-law, Sara and Ned Dulla till 1:30 am. After they all left, he remembers drinking milk and talking to the victim. Remembers his eyes getting heavy. Realized he had fallen asleep when he was woken up by Monica Mehta at 5:50 am.
- Activity report between 2:00 am and 4:00 am – sleeping.
- Alibi – none.
- Any Motive for wanting victim dead – yes.
(a) To acquire victim's assets, that were to go to him as per her will.
(b) He has a reputation of a Casanova, may have fallen in love with someone else.
- Rapport with victim – Was victim's childhood friend. It is believed that he loved her.

7. Mr. Yuvraj Mehta

- Relation to the victim – Brother-in-law.
- Age – 24 years.
- Last saw the victim alive at 1:30 am.
- Went to bed at 1:45 am
- Activity report between 12:30 am and 2:00 am – Was

with his brother and the victim till 1:30 am. Went to bed after that.

- Activity report between 2:00 am and 4:00 am – sleeping.
- Alibi – none.
- Any motive for wanting victim dead – no.
- Rapport with victim – was victim's best friend.

8. Mr. Ned Dulla

- Relation to the victim – Ex-Fiancé and family friend.
- Age – 27 years.
- Last saw the victim alive at 1:30 am.
- Went to bed at 1:40 am.
- Activity report between 2:00 am and 4:00 am – sleeping.
- Alibi – none.
- Any motive for wanting victim dead – yes.
- (a) Didn't appreciate the victim breaking off their relationship.
- (b) His twin sister Sara Dulla was engaged to Siddharth Mehta four months ago. The engagement was broken and Siddharth got involved with the victim. He may have been bitter about this.
- Rapport with victim – was cordial with the victim.

9. Ms. Sara Dulla

- Relation to the victim – Siddharth Mehta's ex-fiancée and victim's friend.
- Age – 27 years.
- Last saw the victim alive at 1:45 am.
- Went to bed at 2:00 am.

- Activity report between 12:30 am and 2:00 am – Was with the bride and groom till 1:30 am. After everyone left them alone, she went to the kitchen to get milk as per Hindu wedding rituals for the groom. She gave the milk to the victim at 1:45 and went to her room. Her sister's twins were sleeping in her room.
- Activity report between 2:00 am and 4:00 am – sleeping.
- Alibi – none.
- Any motive for wanting victim dead – yes.

(a) She was engaged to Siddharth Mehta four months ago. The engagement was broken and Siddharth got involved with the victim. She had a nervous breakdown at the time of the breakup. May have planned it as revenge.

(b) Was visiting a psychiatrist, as per the doctor she is still not mentally stable.

- Rapport with victim – was apparently friendly with the victim.

10. Twins Jack Mehta and Jill Mehta (5 year old), children of Mr. Vikram Mehta, were put to bed by their aunt Sara Dulla at 12:15am. They slept with her in her room.

11. Servants
   i. Harsh Sharma – man servant/butler (65 years)
   ii. Sudha Rani – cook (39 years)
   iii. Gita Devi – maid (19 years)
   iv. Mita Kumari – maid (29 years)
   v. Ram Malviya – gardener (57 years)
   vi. Upma Singh – maid (40 years)

Servants i) to v) went to the servant's quarters at around 12:50am, after receiving gifts from the newly married couple and clearing up after puja. All of them went together.

Upma Singh came a week before the marriage as an additional help. She didn't have any sleeping quarters, so she slept in the kitchen. She was going out to the servant's quarters to get ready for the day at 5:30 am when she recognized the victim's wedding dress from afar. She went to the pavilion and discovered the body. She ran back to the palace and met Yuvraj Mehta coming down the staircase. Yuvraj inspected the body, then woke everyone up and called the doctor.

Police Findings
1) Sleep inducing drug found in the glass of milk which Siddharth Mehta drank, prepared by Sara Dulla.
2) An ear-ring found on the Pavilion. Identified as the one being worn by Sara Dulla on the wedding day.
3) Potassium Cyanide wrapped in a paper found in Sara Dulla's room.

Suspect as per facts:
As per police findings, forensic reports and witnesses' statement, Ms. Sara Dulla is the prime suspect and the court is requested to issue a warrant for her arrest.

***

"We are going to give this report to KD Mehta!" Sub Inspector Madhur exclaimed. He looked at his colleague as if he had lost his mind. "We can be suspended for this!"

Sub Inspector Sharma shook his head, "This is not a regular case, Madhur. We are dealing with the Mehtas."

"The Mehtas move in the high profile circle of Ratnagiri but that doesn't make them any special than the rest."

"You are new here so you don't know what they have given this town," said Sharma. "Before the Mehtas came here we only had a small market, a rickety central road and far flung hill hamlets to call a town. Then Mrs. Mehta acquired the hundred acre property and changed this town for good. The old Ratnagiri Palace and the grounds surrounding it were restored as a family home and the other hill covered by the Sal forest was converted into a world class Destination Spa..."

Madhur cut him off mid sentence, "Ratnagiri was obviously an ideal location for their purpose. They didn't do all this because of some altruistic reason." Madhur shrugged offhandedly.

"Today Ratnagiri is known for its high society, gaiety balls, gymkhanas and opulence. This is all because of the Mehtas. They gave our town a prominent place on the map of India by building one of the world's best spas and a resort here."

Madhur was still not impressed.

"You are not looking at things from the perspective of us residents, Madhur," Sharma explained patiently. "Thanks to the advent of tourism the town now attracts tourists from all over the world and the natives of Ratnagiri who had followed the agrarian way of life earlier are presented with new avenues to make their living. Old houses are converted into hotels and restaurants. Picnics are organized by the locals for the tourists in the adjoining woods along with trekking for adventurers. Handicraft industry has flourished," he paused for breath. "Ratnagiri has prospered because of the Mehtas." Sharma stressed, "We owe them our loyalty."

"Does loyalty mean covering up their crime?"

"Of course not," Sharma was taken aback. "We will just try our best to co-operate with the family and be discreet in our investigations. Mr. KD Mehta gives great credence to discretion," he added reverently.

"What about the victim's family?" asked Madhur. "They also wield quite a bit of power here. Aren't they going to pressurize us in some way to get to the murderer as soon as possible?"

"The Rathode family is least bothered about Gulab's murder. The girl wasn't really close to them. As far as they are concerned she is as good to them dead as she was living. But yes, the public's interest in this case has mounted because of the victim's association with a family of clout."

Madhur nodded. "So, are you also planning to help the Mehta's by pinning this crime on that girl, Sara? She isn't a Mehta, that's why?"

"She may not be a Mehta but she is from the royal family of Ratnagiri."

"She is a Royal?"

"Yes. His Highness Dilip Dulla and his British wife had three children. Their elder daughter Monica and twins Sara and Ned were born and brought up in London. His Highness died seven years ago and a year after his death Mrs. Dulla brought Monica to India to find a suitable match for her as requested by her late husband. She settled down in Ratnagiri and renewed her bonds with Mrs. Sarojini Mehta. Always one to further the interests of the family, Mrs. Mehta arranged an alliance between her eldest grandson Vikram and Monica Dulla, inviting royal blood into their lineage. Following Mrs. Dulla's death last year, the twins returned to their motherland for good."

"The Dullas are involved in some kind of construction business, aren't they?" Madhur was curious.

"Yes. Ned Dulla has a degree in Management from Yale University and heaps of maternal money. He bought a stake in his uncle's thriving construction business in India and settled on the outskirts of Ratnagiri along with his sister Sara Dulla, in their ancestral farm house."

"You really believe Sara Dulla is the murderess?"

"She did have motive, means and opportunity." Sub Inspector Sharma considered for a minute. "But so did others who were present in the Palace that night," he rubbed his forehead. "We can't make conjectures in these high profile cases. We have to tread very carefully as both the press and public will be following every move of ours. But we *have to* find some answers soon as the revised official report is to be filed in by the month end."

Madhur exclaimed, "Fifteen days is all we have!"

A Cortege of Mourners - 2

I

Ned had just come back from the Ratnagiri Palace. His head was throbbing with a dull and steady ache, begging for relief. He had popped in a few pills to induce sleep which had been evading him for days but sleep was still elusive.

He fell back on his favourite rocking chair, it creaked under his weight. Ned had a toned body, lean but tough. Not very tall, both Sid and Yuvraj towered over him. He took out his lighter from the breast pocket of his pin-striped suit and lit a cigarette. Looking into the cloudy fumes emanating from his nose, his vision as hazy as the events of the past few days, his mind drifted over them restlessly.

Gradually, an hour later, the gentle motion of the chair lulled him into a light slumber.

As it happens so often, the world of dreams open their doors to us and we know it's not reality but just our subconscious playing games with us. Ned knew it was a dream. A dream so vivid that it could have been real had he not known better.

"Rose!" he breathed.

She had her back to him, an apparition in white but he could recognize her somehow. Her skirts flowing around her, she was moving away from him. He didn't dare move for fear that he would wake up. He wanted to see her face again, breathe her scent once more and listen to her say his name just one more time. Suddenly she turned. Her hazel eyes blinked at him. He had always thought her eyes to be her best features, green flecked with gold.

Once again he breathed, "Rose!"

Rose was not exactly beautiful when alive but when this vision smiled at him, he saw gliding towards him the most beautiful woman he had ever seen. Death becomes her, he thought with a sad smile. Her wispy dress with a plunging neckline, flaunting her star shaped pendant, slithered on her. Her bangles were clinking together; a sound which Ned had always adored. She glanced languorously towards him as if whispering her longing for him. Reaching him she held the arms of his rocking chair, stopping its motion and moved closer to him. She bent to look into his eyes and Ned could smell the whiff of her perfume as she touched her lips lightly to his ear. She was about to say something in his ear when the buzz of the phone pulled him out of his dream mercilessly.

He opened his hazy eyes to his empty bedroom filled with cloudy smoke from the cigarettes he had smoked earlier, their smell still lingering in the closed room and a little something more. He could pinpoint it at once. Rose's fragrance from the vision still seemed to linger in the room. His vivid imagination was playing tricks with his foggy mind and for a moment he felt still in the grasp of his dream. Maybe it wasn't a dream, he thought indistinctly.

The stale smell of smoke summoned him back to the reality. He swore under his breath and lit a cigarette before picking up the intruding phone.

II

Sara was a petite girl, extremely fair, with a slightly up turned nose and wide set grey eyes. Her jaw line was soft but strong. Her auburn hair was cropped in a pixie hairdo, very short, barely touching her ears. Never one to wear makeup except a smear of a natural lip gloss and small diamond studs always gracing her ears, she was classically simple, an English rose. A soft cultured voice and pleasing manners added to her appeal. The overall effect of her persona was that of a sophisticated young woman.

Sara was a postgraduate in Biomedical Engineering and Regenerative Medicine from University of Leeds. A research scholar, conducting research on cord blood stem cells for her dissertation, she travelled frequently to London. A laboratory was set up in the farmhouse for her use. Usually she spent most of her waking hours in there, but not today. Today she was sitting in her bedroom, her forehead furrowed with agitation. She bit on her lower lip to control her emotional turmoil.

She could not fathom why it was so difficult for people to accept that a person changes with time and so does his feelings?

Her psychiatrist had read to her the work of a French philosopher, Comte-Sponville, and Sara had ridiculed it. He had written:

'Why would I keep yesterday's promise since I am no longer the same today?'

Sara hadn't agreed with Sponville or her psychiatrist back then. But it was not long before her opinion couldn't stay its ground. Her psychiatrist had induced her to read work of philosophers like Aristotle, Peter Abelard, Plato, Augustine and Ayn Rand. Their writings forced her to open her eyes to a totally new perspective of looking at things. She forgave Sid the day she recognized that change is constant and inevitable. She had absolved him of the heartache he inadvertently thrust upon her long ago. She understood that it was not his fault that his feelings for her had changed with time. He was not the same person anymore who had professed to love her last summer.

In the deep recesses of her heart she had always known his truth. She could glimpse a casanova who loved a different flower every season. But Gulab's belief in true love had changed him for good. Sara had always been perturbed by her sweetness, not able to make out if it was just skin deep. But the truth was that she couldn't help but like Gulab. She had thought of all the possible reasons to despise her but could never come up with anything concrete.

So, yes, Sid had left her for Gulab. Had he been the same casanova Sid, Sara would be bitter today. But he wasn't. He was Gulab's Sid. Sara melted into a fit of uncontrollable laugher. The situation was hilarious. Would the police believe her if she told them that her psychiatrist made her forgive Sid?

Yes, she accepted, she had made certain mistakes but who doesn't? If she could forgive Sid why couldn't she, Sara, be forgiven?

All evidence incriminated her. It was as if the cosmos was conspiring against her. How could she make people believe her? Her laughter evaporated into tears of frustration and humiliation.

Sara shivered with an eerie chill in the warm afternoon. She felt goose bumps on her skin, as if a really cold thing was absorbing her warmth, leaving behind a cold spot wherever it touched her. She felt a cold weight on her shoulder and shaking the feeling of someone touching her, she left the room to stand outside in the warm sun.

III

"That bitch won't leave us in peace even after reaching hell!" Monica Mehta shouted coarsely into the phone. She was applying nail polish to her perfectly manicured finger nails while talking to her brother. She stopped in her tracks, closing the bottle tightly and banging it roughly on the side table. Her voice had an edge to it, she sounded bitter and vindictive.

Unlike her siblings, Monica didn't have an ounce of her petite British mother in her. Over five feet seven inches tall, she had her father's height, carriage and colouring. Owing to her lanky frame and long legs she seemed even taller standing beside her stout husband. With a long clever face, dark eyes and a wheatish complexion she didn't resemble her siblings in the least. She had a deep adenoidal voice, almost manly in its stentorian tones.

After listening to her brother's response on the other end, her body shook with anger and she barked into the receiver, "Don't ask me to be polite, Ned! Firstly, she bloody well messed your life. Then, thanks to her, Sara had a nervous breakdown. And now to top it all off she is fucking us all from her grave. This investigation can be the end of Sara, you moron, don't you realize it?" Monica had always had an acerbic tongue and she was never afraid to use it on her brother.

Monica's anger subsided after hearing what her brother had to say. She brushed her long chocolate brown hair away from her forehead and affected a voice to calm her irate brother, "I know! I know! Biji won't let anything happen to her."

"I was relieved when she drew her hooks off you. And God has saved us a second time too. She would have made a terrible wife for Sid," after a pause she added slowly, "Vikram was devoted to her. I hated it. Simply, hated it," upon taking her husband's name her voice softened but the menace in her eyes doubled. Monica was a very jealous woman, more so where her chubby husband was concerned.

"I swear, I would have murdered her myself rather than accept her as family!" her dark eyes oozed hatred.

She listened for a minute to what Ned said, then cut him off and said in an apologetic tone, "Ok! Ok! I won't say such things," she looked around her, "I didn't actually murder her!"

Unlike her voice her expression wasn't apologetic in the least. After a few more minutes of conversation, she put down the phone.

Thinking about Gulab gone forever, her lips curved in a satisfied smile. She had got what she wanted, at last.

IV

Siddharth Mehta was sitting on his writing table, searching for his old books of poems. He hadn't needed them for quite some time for he had a great memory and didn't forget a poem once read. Sid used to take poetry as just a means to impress people around him, especially the fairer sex. His ability to remember and quote the work of famous writers at the right time gave him an edge over the other suitors who lacked his style and flamboyance. William Shakespeare, Emily Dickinson, William Wordsworth, Robert Frost and Oscar Wilde's words seemed to be a part of his very vocabulary. The poignant words of the masters in his deep voice weaved a magical web around the listeners and drew at the strings of the coldest of hearts.

His soulful eyes were the colour of burnished wood. His good looks were accentuated by his straight nose, brown curls, strong build and a height of over six feet. The face etched in the mould of Eros with high cheekbones and broad forehead gave him a boyish charm. A scar near his eyebrow was the only sign of his mortality, marring the otherwise perfect face. His preferred style of dressing was semi-casual, trousers, polo-necks and casual coats. His curls were always jelled, giving him a wet tousled look.

Sid was baffled today. He couldn't remember anything, neither sonnets from Shakespeare nor poems of Kipling. Even Christina Rossetti's songs eluded him. He felt lost in a sea of words. They teased him by nagging at his memories but as soon as he reached for them, they dodged him. The sea transformed into a desert, a never ending desert. He realised that he could not escape it ever. His mouth felt parched, throat dry. He was looking around like a lunatic for what he truly desired. He reached a tent at last. All kinds of mouth-watering meals were available there. There was juice, soft drink and his favourite scotch. But he just wanted a sip of water. His urgency to find water increased.

Shouting "Water, water. ....water" he woke up.

Overpowered by the dream he sat still, absorbing his surroundings, the books around him. He remembered wanting to look up a poem. After Gulab's death, he had drowned himself in reading his old books. They kept his mind off her. For the first time in his life he was interested in these books for something other than wanting to impress people. He rubbed his eyes and got back to the task at hand. He picked a thick leather bound volume and opened it. It opened up to a dried up flower placed between the yellow pages. He remembered the once bright red rose he had kept there as a souvenir. It was from *her*. Her memories flooded his mind once again and a spur of words by Emily Dickinson resonated in the close confines of the room.

'Heart, we will forget him,
You and I, tonight!
You must forget the warmth he gave,
I will forget the light.

When you have done pray tell me,
Then I, my thoughts, will dim.
Haste! 'lest while you're lagging
I may remember him!'

V

A tall man in his late fifties with piercing brown eyes and a distinguished personality alighted from the Mercedes S Class. A hooked nose and a strong chin reflected his arrogance and a quick stride and toned body belied his age. A neat touch of grey at the temples and thin rimmed glasses on his nose were the only indication of his true age. Strict timelines, healthy food and pursuit of his passion to make more and more money kept him in this immaculate shape. A brilliant business sense combined with razor sharp memory and intellect par excellence made him one of the most successful business magnates of the country. His paternal money had helped his father start this business half a century ago. After his death, his mother's hard work and tenacity helped it flourish. But K D Mehta's golden touch was the reason behind the exponential growth of the Mehta Empire.

Unlike his wife, KD was an early riser. His day started at five in the morning. After an hour long jog, a full breakfast and an hour with the newspapers, his work began. He travelled extensively and rarely sat in his office even when in town. He was never home for lunch. But today was an exception. He wanted to have a chat with his son, Sid. He was sad for Sid's loss but being a practical man he decided it was time he cleared a few financial and legal matters with him.

He went directly to the dining room where Sid was waiting for him. Sid was heading the sales section of their family business. He had a way with words and was extremely persistent. These qualities made him excel in his chosen field.

KD entered the dining room through an arched grand entrance. He joined his son on the table and came straight to the point.

"You knew about Gulab's will?" he asked.

Sid's mind blanked for a moment at her mention. Then guilt surged in his blood almost instantly. After a minute he answered, "What will? I don't think she made one," he took a sip of water from his glass not meeting KD's eyes.

KD persisted in an interrogatory manner. "Think carefully."

"Dad! What's the point of this interrogation? I don't appreciate it," he replied irritated and got up to leave the room. Generally calm and composed, Sid was edgy since the tragedy.

"Inspector Sharma called today. Apparently Gulab made a will when she turned eighteen and inherited her mother's estate."

Sid had reached the door but this gave a pause to his flight out of the room.

KD continued in his deep penetrating voice, "It was in your favor, Sid. And her stepmother says you knew about it."

Sid turned towards him with the door ajar.

"What! But....but that was a joke, Dad!"

His surprise didn't seem genuine to KD. He questioned once more, "Really, son?"

"Yes! We made wills in each other's favor as a joke. I never knew she followed the legal proceedings. I was trying to get back with her after our break up. I wrote a will with the forged signature of witnesses in her favor and gifted it to her. It was to signify my commitment to her. Just a gimmick, Dad. And she followed suit," he clarified, albeit a trifle hastily.

"Well, it wasn't a gimmick for her. She did register it," KD shook his head and sighed.

"What of it, Dad?" Sid asked disinterested.

"Can't you put two and two together? It is a lot of money we are talking about here -" KD was about to say more but Sid cut him off angrily.

"You mean to say I murdered her for her fortune," he spoke heatedly. "Do I need her money? Am I not a *Mehta*?"

And to end this discussion as soon as possible he left the room with the door banging after him.

"The police think you are a suspect, do you realize this?!" KD got up and shouted after Sid to grab his attention. "Your philandering ways have caught up with you at last. And that girl should have had better sense. Writing her legacy off to a boyfriend!"

KD had a short temper and he was irked at Sid for not

realizing the gravity of the situation.

Sid entered the room once again and replied with a sad smile, "I wasn't just a boyfriend to her. She loved me, Dad. Even back then. I don't know why or when but she did fall in love with me. And I am lucky that she did!"

Saying this he left the room.

O Innocent Victims of Cupid

I

I *don't know how I should introduce myself. Should I say 'I am Gulab' or 'I was Gulab'?*

I am *no longer alive. Grammatically speaking past tense should be used while describing me. Somehow, I don't feel as if I have passed away. I feel so real, just like I used to. Maybe I am more pragmatic now but that doesn't qualify me as becoming a 'was' rather than 'am'.*

So, let me use present tense while talking and reintroduce myself.

I am Gulab Sarin. Gulab to everyone but Rose to Ned.

Sarin is my mother's surname and I have used it since I can remember. Maa was a willful Sardarni from Paonta Sahib, a small town in Himachal Pradesh. She did her schooling from the nearby town of Dehradun and this is where she met my father, Mahen Raj Rathode, a Gahadvala Rajput of Uttarakhand. Against the wishes of the caste conscious gursikh family of my mother and barely tolerating snobbish high profile political family of my father's, my parents married a year after she graduated. My mother was shunned by her family from then on. For them, she died the day she married.

It was not long before my father tired of her. By the time Maa could realize this, I was already on the way. She hoped against hope that things would perk up once I came into the world but the situation never improved. An active member of the ruling party and an aspiring member of the Parliament, my father started distancing himself from my mother. From time to time she heard rumors about his link ups, confronted him but he smooth talked his way out of it all. With time he became less restrained in his affairs and more unconcerned about my mother. When I was two years old, Maa couldn't take his blatant debaucheries anymore and they separated.

Maa settled in Dehradun in a small cottage. As much as I dislike my father I can't say that he was sparing in providing for us. Apart from our cottage in Dehradun, a farm house in Sainik Farms in Delhi, a huge commercial property in Mumbai and a very generous sum of money fixed on my name, was provided as alimony. Within a year of their separation the divorce finalized and we saw in the newspapers the news of my father's second marriage to a wealthy socialite.

Whenever I think of my mother a picture of hers floats before my eyes. Maa sitting on the writing table, facing the open window and wearing a pink salwaar suit. *She always wore Punjabi suits with short* kurtas, *flowing* Patiala salwaars *in plain hues and bright multi-coloured* bandhani dupattas.

I often dressed up like her.

Maa was an extremely attractive lady, gorgeous. I have her heart-shaped face framed by jet black loose curls, big hazel eyes and pouty lips but I can't be described as beautiful. I am at best pleasant looking. I can't remember Maa as being shy and tentative like me but when I get excited and forget my reserve I do metamorphosis into a chirpy girl with an animated voice and dancing eyes, just like her.

I am bequeathed with her willful nature as well and my

destiny was always underlined by this trait. Call me determined or obstinate but I was always able to stretch my hand far enough into the piggybank of my dreams and draw out the coveted ones with ease.

Except my biggest desire.

It didn't slide out easily for me. It was the fattest dream I had ever dared to see.

His name was Siddharth Mehta, Sid for me.

II

I know the exact moment cupid struck my tender heart. As to why I fell in love with Sid, I just have one answer. The winged cupid is blind and the arrow it embedded in my heart had Sid's name on it. I never needed any reason to love him, I just did.

I will always remember the day we first met. It was a long time ago, eighteen years three months and twelve days to be precise.

It was a hot day but school children don't much care if it's too hot or too cold outside, they just like to enjoy their lunch break and play in the grounds as if there is no tomorrow. I think that's the reason why despite it being an extremely scorching afternoon, the school yard of my new school was brimming with students.

I have an urge to delve into my past and relive that day.

What was I feeling back then? Yes, I can still remember vividly.

I am a cute little thing, wearing a yellow frock and sporting two pigtails. I love my new shoes. My Barbie bag, tiffin box and pencil box are also yellow, my favourite colour. All my things are great but this school is not, I sigh. It is my first day here and I am missing all my friends. I hate Daddy and I also hate new mummy. First, Mommy became a shiny star and started living in the sky, away from us. And now Daddy took all my friends away from me. New Daddy who used to live with Mommy said that I had to leave because Mommy wanted me to live with Daddy. But I don't believe it. Mommy didn't tell me once about it. I am her poppet, she always tells important things to me, in my ear. So New Daddy is lying. I hate him too.

I set out to explore the school and maybe make some friends also. Ten minutes later, soaked in sweat and still friendless I accept defeat. A shady tree beckons and tired I decide to sit on its lap, like I used to sit on Mommy's lap. My foot stuck in its roots and I fell, grazing my knee. Howling loudly I slowly get up and dust the mud off my clothes. I look at my smarting knee. It's bleeding. I start crying. I want my Mommy.

"Mommy, send me an angel. I am hurt….an angel ……. ……., " I hiccupped.

This is how he found me in that school yard that hot summer afternoon. A small girl with mud smeared face and big fat tears rolling down her cheeks accompanied by noisy sobs.

"Why are you crying?"

His voice was like sweet honey on a warm toast. It reached me before I could even see his face, a silhouette framed by the sun. I shielded my eyes with my hands, my tears continuing to run in parallel streams from my eyes.

"An..Angel…?" I hiccupped.

"I am Siddharth Mehta, II-A," he replied and bounced next to me on the ground. "What is your name?"

"Gulab Sarin, K G-B."

He looked into my eyes and his small hand reached out to brush away my tears.

"Don't cry, Gulab. My Biji says Santa Clause doesn't bring gifts for crying children."

"Is Santa your friend?" I asked Sid.

"Yes. He brings me toys," he replied.

"Will he become my friend also?" I asked.

"If you become my friend and play with me you can come to my home for the Christmas party and meet Santa," he replied.

"I will." My voice broke again, "But he won't get me toys because I cried."

"You wipe your tears and don't cry ever again. We won't tell him about today. God promise," he crossed his heart.

The little boy with curly brown hair and the sweetest smile I had ever seen winked at me in a conspiratorial way.

That was the exact moment I fell in love with him.

But I am not the only one who has melted like snow, basking in the glory of his love. His smoky eyes and husky voice have charmed many a credulous hearts. I have never been jealous of the rank-and-file of his conquests.

Baring Sara.

She was different. We are so unlike one another yet so alike in certain ways. Both of us have loved and loved dearly. Both of us know by experience that the hardest thing to do is watch the one you love, love somebody else. Someone has rightly said - what is love if not a wild rose with thorns, beautiful and calm, but willing to draw blood in its defence?

Sara did draw my blood but I have eventually forgiven her.

A Family Affair

KD and Vikram were sitting in a discreet alcove in the library, surrounded by old mahogany bookcases placed along the walls, neatly stacked with rows and rows of books. The air inside smelled a bit musty, like an old binding of an ancient book and it comforted KD with its lingering presence.

"I had a chat with Inspector Sharma," he said. "After finding Gulab's will, Sid is one of the prime suspects now."

"Sid didn't do it. We don't have anything to worry about," Vikram replied confidently but with his distinctive awkward half-smile half-frown. He was only pretending to put faith in Sid; inside he was happy about Sid's predicament, wanting him to face the music.

"That's what I am not sure about," KD spoke under his breath.

"What did you say, Dad?" Vikram asked incredulously. He couldn't believe his ears, his father questioning Sid's actions, that was a novelty. Vikram's lumbering manner, awkwardly clutching and un-clutching his fingers, folding and un-folding his legs, and childlike features along with his hesitant voice made him look a little clown like. A little foolish.

His manner repelled KD and he openly showed his criticism

with a look in his eyes and a shake of his head before pointedly looking at Vikram's legs and fingers. Vikram instantly curbed his hasty movements, his expression at once demanding approval and silently shouting his disapproval at being looked down upon. Vikram's rebellion against his father had never been without deference. His mutinous thoughts had never managed to fully kill his desire to be appreciated by his father.

"I asked everyone to meet me in the library at 3:00 pm sharp," KD looked at his watch and finding still five minutes to go, he scowled at it as if reprimanding the watch for being slow and unable to match pace with the mighty KD Mehta.

"Everyone is in the garden for afternoon tea."

The frown on KD's face darkened for he couldn't digest this blatant disregard of his wishes. But before the dam of his anger could break, Vikram witnessed its approach and stopped it in tracks by saying:

"Biji's orders."

This put a valve on KD's ire for he could never disrespect his mother's wishes. He got up with a sigh.

"Let's go out then."

The gardens of the Royal Hill were Biji's pride; she had worked extensively with the landscape designers while forming the initial plans of the gardens and had rigorously monitored their progress over the years. The front gardens were quite formal in layout but the back gardens were an open landscape composed of ornamental shrubberies. Now that she couldn't walk around the grounds Biji had made it a ritual to have tea outside in the tea house where she could see the gentle rolling hills in the vicinity and the breathtaking peaks on the horizon.

KD crossed the living room and through the back door entered the enclosed backyard. Stepping stones leading from the house circled it and extended to the little tea house in the rear. This was where the whole family was gathered for the meeting called in by KD. Sara and Ned were also asked to join in the discussions and they were seated on one side with their elder sister, Monica. The rest of the family members were seated a bit on the other side, making it apparent that the gathering was divided into two groups. Presiding over the table was Biji, manoeuvring her wheelchair right in the middle with the Dullas on her left and Mehtas on her right.

The table was laid for tea and the assembly was partaking of this luscious fare while talking in subdued tones.

As they saw KD's approach, all conversation ceased. KD instantly noticed the division of groups and being the master manipulator that he was, he dragged his seat near the Dullas. KD believed in the maxim of staying closer to your enemies, for there was no doubt in KD's mind that his family came first. It was in the family's interest to have Sara as the guilty party, KD had already decided.

He smiled at the Dullas and nodded his head as if to convey – 'Don't worry, no one blames Sara.' The twins weren't difficult to be taken in by this act but Monica was a different story. Her dark eyes duelled with the darker ones of KD as if saying that she won't be taken in, this was war.

Vikram took a seat near his wife, smiled down at her for a moment before piling up a plate full of treats. Monica looked at him indulgently and filled his cup with hot steaming tea. She was extremely fond and protective of her rotund husband.

Biji asked of her son in her clear, incisive voice, "What is all this about?"

KD replied respectfully:

"Mother, this is regarding Gulab's murder. I wanted us all to understand the situation we are in."

"What situation?" Biji coaxed.

KD sat straight, with his elbows on the table, and addressed everyone at large:

"As you may have realized, all nine of us are suspects of Gulab's murder…"

Before KD could finish the sentence Tina exclaimed:

"Suspects! How can we be suspects?"

KD's sharp eyes drifted towards his wife. Everyone was irritated by Tina's meddlesome habits but no one more so than her husband. He kept on staring at her without saying a word or blinking an eyelid. That was a silent threat meant to scare her off and she absorbed it with a loud gulp. The congregation couldn't decipher KD's silence and Vikram repeated his mother's words albeit a bit slowly, with his mouth full of sandwiches, munching on them between words.

"But….but we all… can't be suspects!" He wiped his lips free of crumbs.

KD got up and looked down sneeringly upon everyone, "Has it never occurred to you people that no one can enter our premise without our permission?"

His eyes passed over an attentive Ned, subdued Sara, vigilant Monica, his intelligent mother, nosy wife, a lost Sid and finally came to rest on Vikram, who had added volume to his mother's interruption a few minutes ago.

His eyes bore into Vikram's questioningly. "Are you really this dense?" he asked contemptuously.

Monica sucked in an angry breath, about to intervene on behalf of her husband, but clenched her lips tight instead when

Vikram shook his head at her. They were a strange couple, both being as diverse as chalk and cheese, yet in many ways perfect. They understood one another very well and there wasn't much they wouldn't do for another; Monica being the overzealous protective consort and Vikram a silent though ardent devotee.

Without waiting for an answer KD's gaze moved on to the Dullas and in a softer tone he continued:

"Guards are on a twenty-four hour vigil on the Palace gates and walls and they didn't report anyone breaking and entering the premises that night. Neither is there any trace of a trespasser found by the police."

After a pause pregnant with sinister connotations, he spoke slowly and menacingly, "Now tell me who did it if not one of us?" He asked of everyone at large but his eyes came back to rest on the Dullas, as if directing the question at them alone and not the whole group.

Monica was quick to retort heatedly, "Why would any of us do it? Gulab was family!"

Her nasal voice sounded more stuffed with the heat bubbling inside her at the unabashed suggestion of KD's eyes.

"Family! You hated her guts," KD laughed mockingly.

"None of us had anything to gain by Gulab's death," Ned was quick to soak up the temperance that Monica was about to exude and spoke very quietly on behalf of his sisters and himself.

KD didn't speak immediately. His suave exterior melted like an ice cube in the hot sun. A nasty smile curved his lips. It made him look like the cunning shrewd fox of a man that he actually was.

"Revenge and jealousy is a good enough motive," his left

eyebrow arched disdainfully, "but let us not get into that. We are not here to discuss motives or throw stones at one another."

He settled comfortably into his seat, folded his legs. "I wanted to keep us abreast of the predicament we are in. We are the suspects of a murder trial," he paused for effect, "And I believe what the police believes. That one of us *is* the murderer," Sara drew in a quick breath and Tina sighed in utter shock. The rest sat open mouthed or wide-eyed, looking at KD in alarm.

He continued:

"I want us all to maintain a solid front and not give in to the urge to backstab each other to save our own asses. If you find out something which can implicate one of us and tarnish our family name, I request you to bring it to me before prattling it to the police. Our aim should be to come out of this tight situation scathe free. All of us should come out scathe free," he emphasized once more, "*All of us.*"

His meaning was clear to all. He wanted to save the pristine image of the family by protecting the family members. Including the culprit. And no one objected to it.

Under the table Sara grasped Ned's hand tightly. He looked at her troubled face and his eyes softened as he held onto her hand in return. A fleeting movement arrested his attention towards the border hedge, his eyes drifting towards the fence. It may have been a slight of his vision, he sighed, upon finding no one there on second glance. But the feeling of being watched from a distance did stay with him, strangely, calming his nerves instead of making him uncomfortable.

"We can survive this situation; together. Are we all in accordance?" he asked with deliberation.

Silence and a nod here and there greeted KD's question and assented their acceptance to his proposal.

"I still can't believe Gulab was murdered," Sid spoke in a flat voice. He hadn't spoken much in the last few days and everyone looked in his direction, concerned. It didn't seem as if he was talking to any one of them. He was looking into the distance, lost in his own world. "Why did she go out to the pavilion in the middle of the night? She would not leave me alone on our wedding night.....No...she can't," he blurted incoherently.

"Who can murder Gulab?" Tina said thoughtfully, looking at her husband for an answer. She was too inquisitive not to put her foot in her mouth. KD shook his head at her for bringing up this question in front of the Dullas.

"Maybe she committed suicide," she offered hopefully after a moment.

"That's what you think?" KD asked mockingly.

"There were no abrasions or marks on her body suggesting struggle. Maybe she just took the poison herself," Tina was quick to clutch at the straw.

"It was her wedding day for Christ's sake and she was ecstatic! Why would she?" Ned asked in a gravelly voice with a bemused expression on his face.

"I don't know! None of us saw her eating something special," she looked around for confirmation and then continued. "How else could the poison have been administered without any fuss?" Tina hedged.

Yuvi spoke roughly with frustration evident in his otherwise fidgety body now tightly curled in the chair:

"In the obvious way!" he shouted, "Someone who knew her well offered it to her, mixed with some innocent looking item. She took it unsuspectingly. How else? You honestly think someone forcefully shoved it down her throat?" There was disdain in his glittering inky eyes.

"It wasn't a suicide," Ned was confident, "the police did not find any trace of poison in her possession, neither in her room nor on her body. If she committed suicide why would she care to hide the poison?" he asked at large.

"Maybe she had kept the poison somewhere other than in her room, took the poison there and then came out for air. Doesn't it happen like that when a rat is poisoned?" Monica offered in her nasally voice, looking at her husband for approval.

Vikram nodded in assent.

Yuvi was incensed by the vile comparison. Her voice grated on his nerves and he closed his eyes for a moment to block it out. He had never liked Monica.

"Sara is a Biomedical Engineer; should know the difference between rat and human poisons. What you think, Sara? A suicide?" Yuvi's addressed Sara but looked at Monica. His voice had challenge hidden in its depths.

Sara spoke quietly in a dignified manner, "Potassium cyanide is a very potent poison and interferes with the red blood cells' abilities to extract oxygen. The victim literally suffocates to death as he breathes in oxygen he cannot use. The effect occurs almost instantly when the cyanide is swallowed, causing immediate unconsciousness, convulsions, and death within fifteen minutes," she continued with threads of pity intermingling with her cool medical explanation, "Even if she wanted to, Gulab...," her voice became brittle as she took her name, almost on the verge of tears, "Gulab couldn't have walked all the way to the Pavilion after consuming the poison. So, she either consumed it on the Pavilion or her body was placed there after she died to avoid detection for the time being. And for sure the poison was administered after we all left," she looked straight into Yuvi's eyes as if claiming points for accepting his dare and concluded, "Yuvraj, you know, I personally think she definitely didn't commit suicide. If she had done so, she was intelligent enough to leave behind a suicide note."

Yuvi averted his eyes from the gathering.

"All this doesn't make any sense," Vikram's eyebrows furrowed in thought. He stopped stuffing cake clumsily into his mouth and looked around the table. Monica nodded at him in support, her hand patting his arm soothingly.

"All this will make sense if the person who did it comes forward," KD said empathetically. His glance slid towards Sara, the insinuation clear in his voice. "In confidence, of course and confess. We will find out a way to help without going to the police," KD laid the trap.

Ned was quick to get his meaning and he responded with passion, "Sara didn't do it! I would not advise you to insinuate it again," the threat in his voice was clear.

KD raised his eyebrows and said mater-of-factly, "I never said she did. Though the police found the poison in her room and her ear-ring was lying next to the body," he was nonchalant in this claim and looked away into the distance.

Ned stood up at once and Sara and Monica followed suit.

"Good to see you, Biji," Ned said softly, with a slight bow, and all three of them left the table without saying another word. Monica looked back at Vikram for a second before entering the Palace, her eyes passionately loving. The extent of her feelings for her husband was nakedly displayed for that second, for anyone to witness, before she hid them behind the cloak of care and comradeship.

Looking after their retreating figures, Biji asked sharply:

"Are you sure Sara did it?"

KD took some time in replying.

"I just wanted to disconcert them," his eyebrows drew together in thought. "Too bad the servants have been with us for years," he shook his head and stood up to walk around the table.

He spoke to himself, "Actually, any one of us could have done it."

He saw five expressions break up - waver. He saw fear - comprehension - indignation - dismay - horror, but he saw nothing definitely helpful. The tea cup in Tina's hand wobbled upon hearing this, spilling some tea over the saucer. KD was quick to catch her disconcerted act and eyed her from under hooded brows.

"Dad! Don't say such things. None of us had anything to do with the murder," Vikram said, rubbing his hands agitatedly.

"Talk about you, not everyone else," KD said scathingly. "I don't trust anyone of you, specially your wife. She was all out for Gulab's blood. And she is one relentless and vindictive woman," his eyebrow arched for effect.

"She didn't do it. She was with me the whole night," Vikram interjected defensively. His voice was filled with anger and this time he was not afraid to show it. His eyes duelled with his father's and came out victorious.

KD shrugged his wide shoulders, "Better tell her to stick her loyalties to us then. That is for her own good," he ordered, with innuendo lining his words.

He next shifted his eyes to his mother, taking in her proud and arrogant demeanour.

"Mother wanted Sara to be in Gulab's shoes," he tapped

his fingers over the table, "Think I don't know that?" he asked softly of his mother. "And I also know that Mother will anyhow get what she wants," he smiled cockily at her. Biji smiled back without saying another word, silently looking over her son.

He continued deprecatingly with his crooked smile intact:

"And whatever I may say, professionally speaking, I am nothing but happy with Gulab gone. She had not yet taken over Vikram's project from us and now never will," he smiled devilishly.

Vikram sucked in a heated breath upon being reminded of the futility of his dreams, lost forever with Gulab gone. His gaze as he looked at his father was filled with hatred.

"So, maybe you didn't kill her, Vikram, but what about us all?" KD's eyes shifted once more to his eldest son who had for once forgotten about the food on his plate.

KD plummeted back on the chair with the grace of a cheetah. He settled into the soft cushions, dropped his head back and closed his eyes. His leashed power was visible even in his relaxed posture. A master at deceit he was ready to spring at his prey once it lowered its guard.

He opened his eyes and surprised a small smile on his son's lips. Finding KD's eyes on him, Vikram's expression changed instantly and he said in a hustle, "Dad, all this may be true. But that doesn't mean that any of us can commit a cold blooded murder."

"My dearest son, you still have quite a bit of money of Gulab's in your business account. Now that you can't buy out The Mehta Group's shares with that limited amount, what will you do with it all? Her money can only do you good, my boy. Moreover she was becoming quite a pain to you, wasn't she?

Can't you have killed her then?" he asked with deliberation, nodding his head from side to side.

"Dad!" Yuvi screeched, horrified, "How can you say all this?"

KD laughed cruelly with his head thrown back, enjoying everyone's discomfit and continued:

"Vikram's darling wife's position in the society is not threatened anymore by the much more beautiful, intelligent, rich and well connected sister-in-law. Vikram gains to profit a lot by his partner's death. Sid has inherited all of his dead wife's property. Sara and Ned have had their revenge. Tina and Yuvraj can easily be accomplices to any one of us and Mother can now marry her dearest grandson to the girl of her choice," the decibels of his angry voice increased with every added word.

A bit out of breath, he stared everyone in the eye and dared them to refute his claims. Sensing their uneasy acceptance he gave in, his stance relaxed, he exhaled his anger and settled in his seat once more.

"All hypothetically speaking, of course," he smiled his famous lopsided crooked grin.

"Someone amongst us *is* the murderer. It had better be Sara than a Mehta, though I have my doubts as to that," he shook his head at them all. "Time is of essence here. Till now the Police have stoically maintained that we are above suspicion but they can't keep it wrapped up for us for much longer. Inspector Sharma is going to submit a report to the Police Commissioner after fifteen days and the press report will also be released the same day."

His eyes hardened, "I *will not* accept 'a Mehta' being looked upon as a murderer. I *will not* let the press trash our hard earned pristine public image. I *will not* tolerate the people who have always looked up to us daring to badmouth our name," his nostrils flared violently. "We are the Stars, the invincible, and we will forever remain that." He threw back his head arrogantly.

"Let the countdown begin. KD Mehta has never backed down from a challenge yet and never will." His eyes burned with resolve. "Even if it means incriminating an innocent person, I will save our family. Within the next fifteen days."

The Best Mirror

*A*s a teenager I used to devour all the episodes of the hit comic TV series 'Friends'. I fantasized myself as a part of their cool gang and envisaged that one day I would have a happy group of my own as well. But despite this craving, I was never able to form lasting friendships; except Yuvi.

I met him for the first time at his sixth birthday party.

It was a chilly evening and I remember rubbing at the glass window with my gloved hand, the image of a Mickey Mouse etched on the palm, to look out in the distance from the confines of my car. We passed through an ornate gate and drove along the stone causeway. A few minutes later after crossing a bent, nestled in dark trees, a huge grey stone building rose in front of me. It seemed like a fairytale castle from one of my story books.

I alighted from the car holding a brightly wrapped gift and looked around the huge front porch. The figurines of mammoth elephants on either side of the colossal arched wooden front door held me spellbound. A man with a bow tie came down the stairs leading inside the Palace and said:

"Miss, you are here for the birthday party? Please follow me."

I saw huge paintings of frightful men with bushy moustaches and swords in their hands hung on the walls. I was so afraid of them that I decided to look away and in the process my vision *collided with more ghastly creatures, skulls of animals. They had horns and were stuck to the wall. The play of light over them in the dark hallway made them seem fiercer; their big eyes seemed to be looking at me with wrath.*

We had reached the drawing room and I could hear noises coming from within. I stood on the threshold and looked around for Sid in the room decorated with balloons. There was a group of children crowded around a table, partaking of scrumptious treats. Older people were sitting on the sofas and talking. A few of the children were playing some kind of game and I decided to join them. They were holding hands in a circle and singing Ring-a-Ring-a-Roses.

I asked sweetly, "Can I play too?"

A vicious boy replied curtly, "No."

Crestfallen I was standing alone when I felt a tap on my shoulder and craned my neck towards the hand. It belonged to a small boy. Shorter in height than me, he had jet black hair cropped close to his head and big black eyes.

"Who are you?" he looked at me inquiringly.

"I am Gulab, Sid's friend," my head tilted to one side, big golden eyes blinking at him.

I asked after summing him up and finding him likeable, "Who are you?"

"This is my *birthday party," his voice was soft, "You didn't wish me," the small boy said accusingly.*

"I got you a gift," I hedged and proffered the gift towards him.

Ignoring the gift, he retorted sullenly:

"Want to be wished 'Happy Birthday'." His habit of speaking in short, crisp half sentences had been with him even then.

"Happy birthday!" I prattled, making a face at him.

The shrieks of the children playing in the garden caught my attention.

"Let's play with them," I said.

"They won't play with us," his face dropped.

"Why?"

"They are Sid's friends, not mine" he said sadly.

"But they came to your birthday party," I pointed out, "You are a good boy, you can become their best friend."

"No, they won't let me."

"Oh!" I nodded thoughtfully, sad for him.

"We can be friends, if you want." Hearing this, his eyes lit up with hope.

Yuvi took me to look around the Palace. This time the horrid creatures on the walls didn't look so frightening to me and the hallways seemed brighter too. And from then on Yuvi became my best friend.

As a teenager I was a happily plump girl, shy and reserved, with a hipster style and a passion for reading and writing. I dressed with a spirit of abandon, so unlike my tasteful family, in torn jeans, handmade tie-died T's and long colourful flowing skirts, loose long hair tied with Pocahontas headbands and painted my nails black and blue. I also wore Patiala suits like Maa quite often though they were not in rage back then. My huge eyes were always kohled; I preferred cheap imitation jewellery, nose rings and glass bangles. In short I was the resident weird girl of Ratnagiri. But Yuvi didn't care.

I never had to speak to be understood around him. He teased me, guided me and listened to me rant and rave. It was Yuvi whom I called when I fought with Sid and again when we made up. It is said that the best mirror you can have is a true friend.

Yes, Yuvi was my best mirror.

Double Trouble

"You will get your money back within a month," Sid spoke slowly through clenched teeth. "I can't draw it out yet. *She just died.*" He looked around furtively for any eavesdroppers.

After listening to the response on the other end, his expression changed instantly. A look of dread entered his eyes and his voice took on a placating note.

"I am in a situation here; please understand! It is a murder investigation. I have to be careful," he distractedly combed his fingers through his hair. "Trust me, I will return your money as soon as possible, with interest."

The phone went dead with a muttered threat on the other end and Sid dropped down on the sofa. He was tired of these threats and living in constant fear of his creditors. Decidedly they were not the kind of people he should have entangled with in the first place, he sighed with frustration. He had been praying fervently for this investigation to end so that he can shake these leeches off his back. He cursed himself for the umpteenth time for not thinking through his actions.

"Betting on horses didn't prove too profitable for you?" Vikram came into view from behind the door leading to the dining room.

"Ah…," Sid was surprised at seeing his brother. "It is part of the game." He hedged.

"I have heard from a friend interested in the sport that you suffered major losses," he sat opposite Sid. "Are you planning to ask Dad for the money?"

Sid didn't meet Vikram's eye. "No, I'll manage."

"Gulab's money, humn?"

There was a derisive note in Vikram's voice. Sid's hackles rose instantly.

"Better me than you, using *my* wife's money."

"That's your view point," Vikram crossed his legs, "not mine. I think you should let me use Gulab's money."

"Why should I?" Sid asked with a smirk.

"Because you don't want to be put behind bars for the murder of your wife."

"Have you lost your mind?" Sid stood up at once. With anger evident in his voice he added, "I didn't murder Gulab."

"And I believe you, brother." Vikram smiled up at him, his expression condescending.

Sid was clearly baffled; he continued to stare at Vikram. After a pause, Vikram added:

"Haven't you learned anything from Dad?" he smiled shrewdly at Sid. The wicked smile on his childlike face made Sid reassess the competence of his blundering brother.

"What do you mean?"

"I just mean that you have two options, either you can give me Gulab's money for my project, on loan of course, or use it for your creditors and become the prime suspect for the police investigation."

"The police can never unearth my financial condition. I have a big loop of agents and sub-agents," Sid smirked, "we gamblers operate on our word and not by signed documents. I have more to worry about my creditors who will kidnap me or even kill me if they don't get their money on time rather than the police. They can never connect me with the creditors."

Vikram's eyes gleamed with purpose. He looked pointedly at his cell phone, "These things do have a tendency to come out, sometimes with a little help from an anonymous source."

"You mean to say, *you* will inform the police about my dire state if I don't lend you Gulab's money?"

"Me! I am your brother, how can you even think that?" Vikram's face took on a hurt expression. "But the Dullas can, can't they?"

He added:

"Monica told me that the Dullas are trying their best to wield their influence with the police. They have left no stone unturned in the past five days. Ned even went to meet the Police Commissioner. Don't forget that theirs is a powerful family just like ours. We shouldn't underestimate them. If our secrets are unearthed it will not bode well for us. And you know as well as I do that your secret is better left hidden."

Vikram spoke clearly, in a hardened voice, after a minute of silence:

"Dullas still have ten days before the police submit the investigation report and I am sure they'll do anything to save Sara. But you have only nine days because on the tenth day the Dullas will receive the anonymous call," he paused. "A little embarrassment while asking Dad for a loan for your creditors is all you are going to suffer if you accede to let me borrow Gulab's money. If you don't ...." He shrugged, letting the threat hang in the air before walking away from Sid.

After Vikram left, Sid clutched his head despondently. With the threat of the creditors already weighing him down, Vikram's ultimatum was the last straw. He violently kicked an antique earthen pot shattering it into pieces.

An Accumulated Debt

*I*t was Christmas time once again. I was thirteen years old. Sid had joined St. Peter's School, Dehradun that summer. I had been pacing my room restlessly, waiting for the gift he had couriered for me to the Palace to be delivered. A familiar car carousing our driveway made me rush downstairs in haste. There was a loud bash going on in our living room, which I was industriously avoiding. I always kept away from any party hosted by my family for I was never really welcomed there. I was the rustic daughter of a rustic mother and left to my own devices most of the time. My father considered me a bane of his life and this feeling was absorbed by the rest of my relatives as well.

"Hey weirdo! What are you doing here?"

The strains of music hit my ears and the loud guffaws of my cousins invaded my happy space. Till now I had been so lost in my world that I hadn't really taken in the party going around me.

"Weirdo!" my cousin, Amit, repeated in a jeering voice and his elder sister, Rini, looked me over disdainfully.

"It is Christmas, not Halloween," she added her two cents after examining my clothes and finding them wanting.

I had run out of my room, barefoot, in my excitement. My florescent yellow socks peeked out from under my multicoloured *patchwork skirt almost touching my feet. The pleated skirt and baggy jersey added bounce to my already rotund figure. The Santa cap over my messed up mane had come undone in my haste and was resting loosely over my head. The overall effect was not refined in the least.*

I replied indicating my cap, "I know. That's why the Santa cap."

In response to my cheeky reply, Amit came a little closer and breathed menacingly, "We have our friends here, elegant and high class, not like you and your dead mother. Villagers. Take your sorry ass away and hide in your room, fatso."

Amit was my first cousin, my age and the son my father never had; loved and mollycoddled by him. He was always jealous of my better grades at school and bullied me a lot. My hackles rose at listening to the insult thrown at my mother. I replied sassily:

"I don't even want to attend this drab excuse of a party, dumbo."

I looked disparagingly around at the two dozen kids gathered around the dining table; dancing and laughing.

"I am not dumb!" He breathed fire.

I smiled audaciously, "Your grades tell all."

Amit was about to say something but Rini stepped in. Her head held high and a nasty smile on her lips, she clapped her hands loudly and shouted, "Silence everyone."

Amit hushed loudly to aid his sister and within a few minutes the music had stopped and everyone was looking at the bizarrely dressed girl.

"Let me introduce you to this sorry figure of a girl," Rini pointed her tapered pink nail towards me, "She is the daughter of a countryside woman, who died and left her to fend off her rich relatives. We offer scraps to this little beggar and she survives by

wallowing in them."

She looked contemptuously at me. Being the centre of the attention did disconcert me but I stood my ground without cringing, smiling cockily as if I didn't care. My insides melted in humiliation and shame at not being able to protect my mother's name but I didn't react because I believed that that was what they all wanted.

"Boo-ho, Boo-ho," Amit started booing and others joined him in, jeering at my expense.

Along with the booing, food started landing on me as quick tiny missiles from all directions. I was circled in by the taunting children and couldn't find a leeway to rush to my room. The missiles hitting me didn't stop and I closed my eyes fretfully. Mortified tears welled up in my eyes.

Out of nowhere a thick masculine baritone penetrated my ears.

"Cut out this crap! Right now!" The commanding voice made me open my eyes to see the crowd parting for Vikram.

"Where are your parents?" he asked one of my cousins in an angry voice.

Vikram was an elder in the midst of these children and his ire scared them. Rini replied in a rebellious voice, "We are old enough to party alone."

He stopped in his tracks and stared her down.

"Apparently not," he pronounced.

His voice was miffed and his tall bulky stance managed to cower down the fifteen year old conceited girl and her friends. Vikram reached me and touching my quivering chin made me look into his eyes. His lovingly pulled my cap in place over my unruly hair.

"Merry Christmas, baby," he smiled into my eyes and nodded in silent understanding. He turned me towards the crowd.

"*If any of you ever make fun of Gulab again, I'll snap your backs,*" he roared making the scared children cringe.

Listening to all this commotion, finally my step mother came downstairs. Vikram repeated what had been happening and needless to say, to placate the miffed elder son of the Mehtas, Vina had to take action against the wayward children. The party ended and Amit and Rini were grounded for a week, but not before apologizing to me in front of all their friends.

That was the day I swore on returning the favour Vikram had bestowed on me. I vowed that whatever may befall me, if the day ever arose that Vikram needed me for anything, I would give it to him unreservedly, just like he gave me his brotherly love and support when I most needed it.

And I was blessed the day he finally did come to me for help. I gave him everything he wanted, and more. Had he only decoded my intentions correctly I bet things would have been so different for him today.

Calm after the Storm

"The bottle of saffron is missing from my drawer." Biji frowned worriedly. Biji had summoned Monica to her room as soon as she had woken up in the morning.

"The saffron used to prepare Sid's ceremonial milk?" Monica asked askance.

"What other saffron could I be talking about?" Biji spoke sternly. "I noticed it gone last night."

"Who could have taken it?" Monica clutched her fingers fretfully. "It is dangerous…"

A knock on the door disturbed their solemn conversation. KD entered the room a few seconds later.

"Breakfast is ready, Mother. Care to join us, Monica?"

"I have to wake up the children. I'll join you later." Looking anxiously at Biji and after a curt nod from her, Monica left the room, worry still etched on her face.

Gulab's murder had affected the Mehtas in ways stranger than anyone could have imagined. The family members who hardly saw each other's faces in the course of the usual day were drawn to each other now. Biji who usually had her breakfast in bed was up at the dining table with her son who always had his meal before eight in the morning. Today he lingered at the table to catch his sons. Vikram joined him sometime later. But the surprise package was Tina. Sleep still lurking in her eyes; she joined her family for her morning coffee.

"You are up early, darling? Sleep eludes you too?" KD mocked his wife with his lopsided smile.

"You are late for office, dear. I hope you are not unwell?" She mocked him right back.

KD laughed out loud. This was how the kids had always seen their parents. Casually bantering and teasing one another. They understood each other's weaknesses and accepted them without any reserves. Live and let live was their motto.

"Has anything new turned up?" Tina asked KD.

He sighed loudly. "The case has generated a lot of public interest. I have been following up with Inspector Sharma and he has assured me that he'll do everything possible to help us, provided enough evidence comes up against Sara in the next nine days," he paused despondently, "but if the police are not successful in incriminating her, people will start casting aspersions on us and that won't bode well for the family."

"It's not good for the stock prices of my company either. Gulab's death has already caused quite a stir. Shares are on an all time low," Vikram was upset. He had wagered too high to lose it all now.

"Still considering to part ways, son? I always told you this project has great potential but taking it forwards alone is not a good decision. Moreover you don't have enough money to buy us out now," KD interjected with an arched eyebrow for effect.

"Not a good decision? For me or you, father?" Vikram replied shuffling his feet nervously. He had confidently given an ultimatum to Sid but his insides had melted while doing so.

He hoped against hope that Sid would not discuss it with their father. He broke into a sweat thinking what would happen to his dream project if Sid didn't agree to lend him the money. Taking a deep breath, he resolved to break Sid, come what may.

"I don't think you can find another partner soon. Gulab did have the kind of capital to take over this project but with her gone I doubt if anyone else would be interested."

"Just like you always wanted," Vikram murmured under his breath and subjected KD to a long obscure silent stare from the corner of his eye.

"Let's get back to important matters for now," Biji changed the subject adroitly.

"I saw the police report; they have a very close case against Sara," said Vikram.

"Sara has got nothing to do with Gulab's murder," Biji's voice was firm.

KD's eyes swiftly landed on his mother after listening to the command in her voice. Her eyes dared her son to differ. KD grasped the situation just by looking at Biji's attire. He knew his mother's penchant for mood dressing and her black georgette salwaar suit with small red peonies all over it presented a very aggressive colour scheme. KD could easily glean that his mother had an agenda on hand and was in no mood to give in.

Tapping his fingers on the arm of his chair in a slow tempo, KD spoke meaningfully:

"The police don't think so, Mother,"

"I know what you want them to think, KD. Don't forget I am your mother. You have learned it all from me. Treat both Ned and Sara like family," the threat was clear.

"If you say so, Mother. But then have you considered the

alternative yet?" KD's eyebrows drew together questioningly.

"Neither family is guilty," she replied succinctly in a terse voice.

"Then who is?" KD's voice was drowned in anguish at his mother's bullheadedness.

When Biji refused to answer and just looked through her son haughtily, KD spoke firmly but with a small trace of pleading in his voice, which only his mother could invoke.

"If one of the Dullas is not convicted then a Mehta automatically is! Why can't you see that, Mother?" he reasoned strongly. "Has our family name and honour, which we have striven so hard to create, no meaning for you all of a sudden?" Frustration was evident in his manner, "Even if Sara is not guilty she has to be implicated! *For us all. Our family,*" he stressed, "Is that girl more important to you than your *own family*?" he asked insistently.

"The stakes have been upped, Mother," KD's voice was lined with worry. "This case has started affecting our business now. We lost a contract for the first time in eighteen years. I couldn't believe it at first. If we don't mend this situation fast we will keep on loosing goodwill and new projects."

Without wasting a minute Biji commanded brusquely in a voice which said she expected her orders to be followed, "I can just say that the murder isn't an inside job. Convince the police of the same."

"How should I do that? The surveillance cameras don't show anyone breaking and entering the palace. Nothing has been stolen. What is the motive for an intruder to break in and murder Gulab?" he asked sullenly.

"Do I have to teach you this stuff? Sit with the officer in

charge and work something out for our mutual benefit. If there is no intruder, invent one. If there is no proof, construct some. I thought you were the king of manipulation. Use your ingenuity, my dear. Our coffers have a lot to offer, don't you ever forget that or let the police forget it," she looked directly into his eyes and imitated his son's famous lopsided crook smile.

Her meaning dawned on KD and he nodded, albeit reluctantly.

"I'll talk to Inspector Sharma but I can't promise that our ruse will work," he sighed loudly, "This is not a regular problem; it's a high profile murder investigation," he stressed.

After a minute's thoughtful consideration, he added sulking, "Time is running out, Mother. Nine days is all we have left. Everything will be lost if we follow this path of saving Sara and laying the blame on an outsider, and can't prove it later on," he added a bit more forcefully, "Reconsider, Mother. Please!"

"I know who committed the murder," Tina pitched in a gap in the conversation between mother and son.

All three pairs of eyes zeroed in on her.

"What? Who?" KD and Vikram spoke at once. Their eyes glued to her triumphant face, they waited for her to pronounce:

"Upma."

"Manipulation doesn't mean incriminating an innocent maid. Our servants are old and faithful. This is no way to repay them," ever judicious Biji's voice was gruff, filled with annoyance at Tina's foolish suggestion.

"Upma hasn't been with us for long," she emphasized. "And I am not suggesting you make it *appear* that she did it. I *know* she is the murderess."

"Why didn't you say so before?" KD asked bewildered but with a hint of relief evident on his pleasantly surprised face.

"Because it occurred to me just now!"

"How do you even know?"

It was Sid who asked the question from the doorway. He had entered the room a few minutes earlier and was listening to them all plan and plot behind his back.

Tina couldn't meet Sid's eyes but replied quietly, "Intuition."

"Proof is what the police seek. *Real* proofs," Sid spoke in a slow reprimanding tone, "I hope," he added, looking directly into his father's cold brown eyes. KD huffed and picked up a glass of water to cover the guilt his words brought.

KD was about to say something but Sid cut him off with a hand raised to ward off his words, turned towards his grandmother, stared her in the eye but addressed his father:

"I don't want you to try and save Sara. She killed Gulab and the police have proofs to substantiate the fact."

He advanced towards the table in two long strides. "I will not accept any meddling in order to save my wife's murderer," he turned towards his grandmother and his stance was rigid.

Biji, head held high, wheeled her chair out of the room without speaking a word and KD followed suit. As Vikram passed Sid, he whispered in his ear - "Eight days left, buddy. Decide fast," and left.

Tina got up from her seat and went up to Sid to stress her point.

"I have my flaws, Sid. But I want you to know I didn't just make it up." She added appealingly, "If you just hint it to the inspector, I am sure he will find proofs."

Sid looked at her suspiciously but something in his mother's manner caught his attention and exhausted after this angry tirade he took a seat and exhaled.

"Why would Upma kill Gulab?" his hands flew artistically, rhyming perfectly with his words, like they always did when he talked with passion, "She barely knew her."

Tina sat down on the seat next to him lost in thought for a minute. She said drawing out a tired breath:

"I don't know why, but she did do it." Her voice was vibrating with frustration at trying to make someone believe her but failing miserably in the process.

"Mom, none of us wants to believe that the murderer is one of us," he shuddered with repulsion. "But please don't let all this get to you," he stressed, thinking that her mother truly believing that a servant committing the heinous crime was a subconscious way of her dealing with the unbelievably sticky situation they were presented with.

Sid hugged her impulsively and was immediately smothered in whisky fumes wafting towards him intermingled with a strong perfume.

"Mom! Have you been drinking this early?" Sid asked incredulously.

"I had a couple of drinks last night," Tina hastily pushed him away and poured another cup of coffee.

Both of them were silent for some time, having breakfast, drowned in their own personal thoughts. Tina was just about to leave when Yuvraj came in rubbing sleep off his eyes.

"Good morning, Mom, Sid," he smiled groggily. He looked at Sid with a guarded expression.

"How is my angry young man doing?" Tina asked. "Sleepy head! You have always been a late riser but you have never missed a squash session before," Tina smiled up at him. Her expression changed as an idea hit her and she exclaimed, "Unless your dare devil stunts on that monstrous bike have again resulted in an accident! Are you hurt somewhere? Is that why you slept in?" she got up to check her son's arms and legs for any visible bruising.

Yuvi was known to be a reckless driver and since the day his bike had landed on their premises, he had been embroiled in accidents every few weeks, mostly on the palace grounds trying to perform some stunt. On public roads he always drove with restraint.

Yuvi smiled at her antics and politely drew back from her grasp.

"Haven't had an accident or even a fall in the past six months. Not even a scratch." He asserted, picking up an apple from the fruit basket.

Sid asked:

"Yuvi, are you doing fine? Gulab was your best friend," Sid looked over his brother. He definitely seemed to have withered away in the past few days. His verve was visibly lost.

Some people care and others pretend that they do, Yuvi thought scathingly, upon hearing his brother inquire about his well being.

"Yes," he replied graciously, successfully concealing his true emotions.

"I have noticed you get up late and even sleep in the afternoons. That's not your usual self. She was very close to you but you have to get out of this depression," Sid advised.

"Wrong conclusion," Yuvi replied, succinctly as ever. "Am not sleeping too much or am even depressed. My AC is not working. All that lighting we put up for the wedding has somehow short circuited it. You know how I can't sleep without it. Can't get up in the morning if I sleep late, can I now?" Yuvi clarified in a monotone.

"Call the electrician. Why haven't you?" Tina asked.

"Uh….the wiring is connected to Sid's room. I didn't want to hassle him," Yuvi replied uncomfortably, knowing full well that he didn't mind bothering his brother in the least but he just hadn't wanted to see his dirty conniving face for as long as possible. Yuvi wanted to swear and yell at Sid but he took a deep breath and kept his cool.

"Sleep in the guest bedroom," Tina suggested.

"No," Yuvi replied, a little too briskly.

Sid said, "You can call the electrician. It won't bother me in the least."

Yuvi nodded, not looking directly at Sid.

Sid got up, "I have some work to do. I'll be in the library."

Once alone, Sid weighed his options; to cheat his Dad by giving the money to Vikram or get convicted for the murder of his wife. Both the cases were reprehensible. But what else could he do?

Unless, he thought optimistically, in the next nine days he could prove Sara to be the murderer and hand her over to the police. With the murderer in their custody the police won't care about his creditors and Vikram's threats will lose their hold on him.

He had attempted to dissuade Biji from trying to save Sara. With proofs already piled against her the case could be wrapped up in no time if Biji agreed not to interfere. He just had to find a few more evidences to clinch the case against Sara and get out of this precarious situation scathe free.

Yes, that's what he would do, he resolved.

Sentenced for life

"*I love my girl in pink.*"
"*Ah! Thanks.*"

"*I want you to do something for me, darling…*""

"*If it's not too naughty, I definitely will, love.*"

The screen buzzed instantly with the sound…muaaaahhh… and full red lips appeared on the screen.

"*It was great, baby doll. Loved it. I want to fly to you now. Can't stay away from you for long.*"

"*Waiting for you, honey. And get your web cam fixed soon…. Would love to see you in action…..*"

A few more whispered words were exchanged before the webcam switched off and the screen became blank.

Pink looked good on me and I sported it quite often.

But I was not the recipient of the above compliment.

Sid was in third year at college, doing his five years integrated management course and I was doing my bachelors in economics. I had been studying for my exams and couldn't meet Sid for over a fortnight. I planned to surprise him by going over to the palace unannounced.

I softly opened the door to his room. Taking hushed baby steps I

reached the study table where he was working. I was about to purr
softly in his ear 'Surprise!', when instead of him I was surprised.
The screen of his computer was on fire with a semi clad girl in a
pink shift sitting on a huge bed jamming her hand under the hem
of her tight slip. I was routed at the spot by her explicit actions.
My disgust at her levity was second only to what I could see Sid
typing. Again it was a misconception. What I saw next was the
most nauseating scene of my entire life. The front of Sid's jeans
was open and on display was his naked glory. Alternatively he was
typing and touching that erect mass of his body.

"It's over between us," I remember shouting again and again.
"Don't ever call me again, you scumbag." I curled into a ball on
the floor and started sobbing my heart out. Sid tried to cradle my
body in his arms, I thrashed at him like a wild cat, scratched him,
kicked him, and threatened him not to touch me. More profanity
flowed from my mouth and the fury which boiled inside me made
me an animal. I clawed at his face forgetting that his eyebrow was
pierced. The gold ring he sported tore at his skin and came in my
hand. Hearing him scream and looking at the blood flowing from
his brow I instantly soothed, the pain of being cheated turned into
an ache for his hurt brow.

That was me. Not Gulab but Sid's Gulab. A simple scream of
his and a hint of his pain made me forget the boulder which had
fallen on me unsuspected a few moments ago. I looked closely at
him and he had tears in his eyes mingled with the droplets of blood
flowing down his face. I touched his face softly and said:

"I am so sorry. I'll call a doctor."

I tried to move away but his hand shot out and held my leg. He
crouched before me, holding my feet and in a humble voice said:

"It's hurting, yes. But thousand times less than it will hurt if
you leave me. Please forgive me, Gulab. Please. I promise this won't

happen again. I got carried away in Dehradun. I don't really love anyone except you. It was just physical. I will do whatever you say, but please don't leave me. Please, Gulab. I am sorry."

He visited me the next day and brought with him his will. I knew that it was just a ploy to impress upon me that I'd be his future wife and that sleazy affair didn't matter. I wasn't taken in by the document that wasn't even legal but was happy that he cared enough to try and mend things between us. I had just turned eighteen and inherited my mother's property. I decided to make my will, the real thing. I didn't do it to score some point with him. I did it because I really believed whatever was mine was his too.

I don't want to give the impression that it stopped hurting after his heartfelt apologies and his ardent declarations of undying love. I wanted to forget this whole incident but I never really could, the scar on Sid's eyebrow reminded me of his deceit every time I saw him. The normal trusting girl who had never been prone to suspicion earlier was now transformed into an ever suspicious spy, fiddling with Sid's phone, his emails, and his diaries, anything I could lay my hands on. I was always on my feet, ever watchful.

But I never ceased to love him.

I had accepted my sentence; to live and die a prisoner of his love.

Masked Devils

L aughter wafted all around the Ratnagiri Palace, uninhibited and joyous. It did not recognize the need for subtlety for it couldn't appreciate death as the life stealing pandemic it actually is. Children accept things at face value. Aunt Gulab was in heaven now. She may be the new tooth fairy, Jack and Jill reasoned. Obviously when their teeth would break she'd come and meet them. They had lots and lots of teeth, both of them. Aunt Gulab would visit them often enough.

The thinking of five year olds was so uncomplicated. They accepted change willingly. Letting go was so very easy for them.

Jack and Jill couldn't understand why the elders seemed so gloomy. Maybe because all their teeth had broken years ago, when they were children, Jack offered. Maybe they all had false teeth like Biji's, Jill added. But both of them were still young and of course when Aunt Gulab came to meet them, she'd say hi to everyone else too. Elders were so dumb. They nodded their heads in unison.

They were playing their favourite new game; Ghost – Ghost.

Draped in a stole around their head and shoulders, a long scarf tied around their hands, fingers wrapped together as one and the thumb wrapped separately, they tried to scare anyone within range, the family, servants or each other.

"Jack, let's scare Grammy," Jill suggested animatedly, tiptoeing from one foot to the other in her excitement.

Treading softly into the living room, both Jack and Jill, pounced on their unsuspecting grandmother with a gut wrenching screech and presented her with the view of their supposedly monstrous claws.

Taken aback by the noise, Tina dropped the magazine she was reading, "Good God!"

Though she had been surprised into getting scared, the adorable expressions on the chubby innocent faces of her grandchildren appeased her instantly.

"Grammy! It's us, don't be afraid!" Jack immediately tried to soothe her and picking up the magazine offered it back to her.

"Stupid! You were not supposed to tell her about us! Now, she'll tell everyone we are the ghosts and no one will be scared of us," chest heaving, hands on her waist Jill breathed daggers at her brother.

"But Jill, Grammy was really afraid," Jack said placating, with a considering look towards his beloved Grammy.

"Hey! Why are you guys making such raucous noises?"

Sid had been working in the library and distracted by the noise he came looking for its source.

"We are ghosts. We'll eat you alive," Jill added a sinister intonation to her voice and started moving towards Sid, her claws on display. Jack followed suit.

"Yes, we are here to take you with us to the...ghost... world," Jack tried to mimic his sister.

Feigning terror and slowly pacing back towards the wall in mock fright, Sid begged, "Please ghosts! Please don't eat me. I am a good boy."

"We spare people who get us chocolates. Will you get us one?" Jill asked, still wielding her scarf clad claw.

Pretending to be scared stiff, and in no situation to bargain, Sid replied tearfully, "Yes…yes, I will get you chocolates. Now please spare me."

"It's us, Uncle Sid. Jack and Jill," Jack laughed.

Their curly heads bounced as they jumped and screeched.

"We fooled you! We fooled you!"

"Oh! It was you guys! I could never have guessed."

"Don't you encourage them, Sid. They have been disturbing everyone with this terrible game for days now," Tina reprimanded.

"And you little devils come here. Sit with me," she tapped the sofa next to her.

Both of them sat on either side of their Grammy. She reprimanded but gently, "You are acting like fools, children. Everyone knows you are not ghosts. So, quit playing this annoying game."

"You were afraid of us, Grammy," Jill insisted obstinately. "You thought we were ghosts."

"I was just surprised!" Tina exclaimed.

"Do you think we are not ghosts because we are not tall?" Jack asked innocently.

"Tall? Anyone can see that you are Jack and Jill!"

"But Grammy, we are wearing two masks," Jack stressed. "See," he stretched out his hands tied with the scarf and pulled at his stole.

"It's not a mask, honey. It's a scarf and a stole."

"Jack, I told you the colour was wrong. It is like skin colour but you wouldn't listen to me. Stupid! Stupid!" Jill crawled over her grandmother's lap to reach Jack.

"You stupid! Ghost can tie hand with any scarf. Stupid!" Jack retorted.

"No. It is special scarf like skin, like Biji wears on her legs. I know it. Stupid," Jill shouted back and pulled at Jack's hair. Jack followed suit. Within no time the fight went out of hand and both started crying.

Sid immediately separated them and took Jill off her grandmother's lap. Tina soothed Jack.

"I ha…hate you," Jack cried.

"I won't talk to you," Jill cried back.

It took some time to control them both. Sid patted Jill and said, "Jill, you pulled at his hair first. You should apologize to Jack."

"But Uncle Sid, he spoiled our mask," Jill looked at Sid with her tear strewn face.

"What mask, Jill?" Sid asked frustrated.

She proffered her hands clad in scarf which had got untied in the scuffle.

"I told Jack that ghosts don't wear colourful scarves," she offered tearfully, "but, he didn't listen. Now, everyone knows we are not ghosts. Because of him!" She pointed a plump finger towards the aggrieved Jack and tried her best to reach him and strike again, but Sid easily controlled her, pulling her tightly back on his lap.

"But, the ghost I saw didn't wear Biji type scarf," Jack offered snivelling.

"When did you see this ghost, Jack?" Sid asked angrily, he decided to put a lid on this play acting even if he had to use a little force.

"The same night Aunt Gulab became a tooth fairy. Aunt Sara saw it too," Jack replied with conviction.

Sid couldn't make sense of this childish conversation. It may have been a game invented by Sara, he thought.

"Liar! Aunt Sara didn't see the ghost," Jill made a face at her brother.

"She saw it! At night she slept with us!"

"Ghost came in the morning and Aunt Sara was sleeping!"

"At night!"

"In the morning!"

"Stop it you two!" Tina scolded them. "Run off to your Mum. You have given me a headache. Off you go!"

Still fighting it out, the scuffling children took their leave to play some more in their play room.

"Devils!" Tina sighted tiredly.

Sid looked after their retreating figures contemplatively. Children were so funny, living in a make believe world of their own, he thought. He would have loved to possess this quality too. Life would become much simpler, he sighed.

"I need a martini. Shall I pour you one too?" Tina asked moving towards the bar.

"You want a drink before lunch?" Sid had never noticed his mother drinking in the day. But before now their daily routine hadn't been the same. He was never home and neither was his mom.

"Just a cocktail," she replied flippantly.

"Has your father talked to Inspector Sharma about Upma?" she asked with her back to him.

"I don't know," Sid replied. "Mom, this is a strange fixation of yours."

She gulped down her drink and with heat in her voice replied, "She killed your wife! Will you not punish the woman who took Gulab away from you?"

"Why would she kill Gulab? You are paranoid!" saying this he walked out. He realized that his mother wanted to pin down the murder on an unconnected party to end it all. Upma was the only servant who was new to the palace, the rest of them were a brigade of old and trusted employees who had earned Mehtas' trust over the decades. So, Upma it had to be.

His mother needn't worry anymore, Sid thought. He had already concocted a plan to incriminate Sara further and himself ease away from this situation. The plan did have the potential to backfire. Was the risk worth the result, he sighed agitatedly, his anxiety increasing with every step he took. At last, strengthening his resolve he drew in a deep breath and picking up the phone, dialed a number:

"Inspector Sharma? Siddharth Mehta this side. I have some important information for you...."

Forget-me-not

It was the day my life took a turn towards Mumbai. I was pacing frantically, waiting for Sid to meet me at the Pavilion when I saw Yuvi walking towards me.

"Saw you from my balcony," he spoke without preamble, a frown etched on his brow. "Seem worried? Had a fight with Sid?"

I rushed to his side and clutched his hand agitatedly. "You remember that I had taken the All India entrance exam for a master's course in financial economics?"

He nodded in assent.

"I have received an offer from Salandale. The program on offer is a joint offering by the business school and the economics department of the University."

"That is the most coveted institute of the country, Gulab," Yuvi sounded proud. "I believe they take only the top forty students each year. You should be happy."

"I know. I know," I held my head anxiously in both my hands and started pacing again. "It would have been the happiest day of my life had the university not been in Mumbai." I rambled on, "Amit, my cousin, had also taken the exam and his score is below average…."I exhaled loudly, not clear how to express myself, "I have always wanted to prove my worth to my father and his

horrible family and this is the perfect opportunity. All the slights I have endured over the years at their hands…. today can be my day… But how can I leave Ratnagiri…I can't…"

"Gulab! Stop this right now." Yuvi pulled me towards him and stilled my frantic pacing, *"Why so flustered?"* he looked at me kindly. *"No one is forcing you to accept the offer. If you don't want to leave Ratnagiri then that's your decision."*

I pulled away from him and resting my back against the balustrade I slithered to the floor, *"I can't live without Sid,"* I leant forward with my head between my knees and mumbled, *"I want to join this course and rub it in my father's face that he had been wrong in discrediting me. I so want to see his family's reluctant admiration for a girl they considered pastoral and unworthy of their name,"* my body shook with suppressed emotions. *"To this day I feel hurt and humiliation at my father not even once suggesting changing my surname to his, following my return to Ratnagiri after Maa's death…"*

Yuvi crouched near me and silently put his arm around me for comfort. I looked at him and my eyes dilated, *"Yuvi, this is my one chance of proving myself worthy of all that I have been denied. And I want to snatch this chance,"* there was fire within me. *"Grab it and walk away with my head held high for the rest of my life."*

He brushed away my tears and sighed with a hint of gloom, *"Go to Mumbai, Gulab."* I gazed in his eyes and could clearly see that he personally didn't want me to leave but was supportive of my wishes. Yuvi was a man of few words, the strong and silent type, but his eyes were very expressive, they never lied. *"You know I can't and that's why I am so upset."*

"Why?" Monosyllables were his favourite even in the midst of emotional discussions.

Beads of sweat formed on my forehead and I rubbed at them distractedly. "I still shudder when I remember those days when Sid was in Dehradun. It is painful to even contemplate not seeing him for months on end," I shook my head, "I know this dilemma will be resolved the minute I look at Sid. After being with him for some time any thoughts of accepting the offer will automatically drive away from my mind. I want to join this course but I just can't...."

My mind was uneasy and rolling with questions, the momentous decision weighting heavy on my heart. I laid my head on Yuvi's shoulder and took refuge in the solidity of my friend, the best listener in the world. He didn't give me any verbal assertions of everything working out just fine but his presence was enough to calm me down. He was a pillar of strength for me.

Neither of us broke the silence till I heard Sid's footsteps from a distance. We got up and Yuvi left me alone with him.

"Hey you!"

I saw Sid walking briskly towards me. His curly brown hair blew with the breeze, away from his face. Eve from a distance I could see his pink smile.

Reaching me in a few quick strides, he hugged me close.

"I have got a call letter from Salandale for my master's course," I said morosely without any preamble, wanting this nagging thorn to get out of the way as soon as possible.

Sid looked shocked and drew away from me at once.

"I didn't apply. Just took the all India entrance exam for our local university," I clarified defensively.

"Hey! I am not angry. I am very proud of you, baby. I always knew you were a good student. But Salandale! Salandale is THE University of India," his expression cleared and he gave me a quick hug.

"I can't go away!" I exclaimed.

"May I ask why?" The smile didn't falter.

"I can't live without you," I hugged him tightly.

Sid tenderly pushed me away and looked me in the eye, "This is your career, Gulab. I can appreciate what Salandale can do for you. I won't ever stand between you and your dreams."

I cut him in mid sentence and asserted, "You are not! I can always study here. Our local college is very good."

Sid shook his head and touched my cheek tenderly, "Don't try to fool me, Gulab. You should go to Salandale! You want to!"

"Not at the cost of leaving you," I repeated with force, shaking my head.

"We have our whole lives to be together. Two years is nothing. I want you to go. Do it for me Gulab Sarin. Please!"

"No…," I said again but the fight was fast draining out of me and I hugged him again.

"I know that I am your priority in life. But, baby, trust me, I will be here when you return. Our love doesn't need constant embraces, we are above that."

I held him tighter and tears which were near the surface spilled over. He pulled away but didn't wipe my tears. He stood there looking at me as if remembering my face. Then he did something which he had never even tried before.

He came very close to me, put his arms around me. His muscled torso rippled under my palms and I felt his heartbeat quicken. He whispered slowly in my ear, as if singing a lullaby to a child and caught me in the web of Robert Dodsley's words weaved with his intoxicating voice.

"One kind kiss before we part,
Drop a tear, and bid adieu;
Though we sever, my fond heart

Till we meet shall pant for you."

After every few words he brushed my tears with his lips and there on my favourite Dancing Pavilion, in front of my friends – the singing birds, dancing trees and cheering flowers, he kissed me like a man for the very first time. My heart fluttered at his nearness, a spark lit my body upon his touch and as soon as his lips touched mine I felt as if I was finally complete. For the next few minutes, embraced in his arms, I danced uninhibitedly. The tempo started with a slow beat and ended with me rotating in circles, arms wide open and head flung back, an expression of pure ecstasy on my face. That is how I have always expressed happiness.

The euphoria of that kiss stayed with me for a long long time. It somehow concreted the foundation of our love. To me it signified the metamorphosis of the verbal assertions of our commitment towards each other to a legal binding deed. I felt like I had somehow bound Sid eternally to me. The thought of his cheating on me again drifted away from my mind. After all, the love and passion in his eyes could not be imitated, I rationalized.

Before I left for Mumbai, Sid would send me flowers every day, always the same flowers. Folklore and legend says that the wearers of this flower would not be forgotten by their lovers. It symbolized true love and memories. And that is what he sent me for each one of the thirty five days I was still in Ratnagiri.

A posy of beautiful blue forget-me-nots.

If Looks Could Kill

The night was still young when Sid came out of his room to join his family in the dining room. He was about to descend the stairs when he saw a beam of light, probably a torch, illuminating Vikram's otherwise dark room. Retracing his steps, he tiptoed to the semi closed door in thoughtful silence. Opening it just a fraction more, he surreptitiously entered, instantly flicking on a switch and lighting up the room with a warm yellow glow.

A small frightened screech greeted his actions and he saw crouched on the floor, furtively opening drawers of the cupboard in the beam of a torch, was his mother.

A hand to her heart, she dropped down on the floor. "Oh! It's you!" She heaved a small sigh of relief upon seeing Sid.

"What are you doing sneaking, Mom?" Sid asked surprised.

Behaving as if nothing was out of sorts, Tina went back to fiddling through the cupboard. She threw back at Sid without taking her eyes away from the task at hand:

"What do you think I am doing?" she asked sarcastically. She shut a drawer noisily and opened the one below it, rummaging in it for a few seconds and then closing it adroitly after she was done. She faced her son:

"Hunt for the murderer is on, my boy!" she added gustily and smiled brightly at Sid. "Come help me," she cajoled. "Turn off the light; we don't want to be caught in action."

"You are impossible!" Sid's gasped with exasperation. "Come with me right now," he commanded his wayward mother.

She got up from the floor and brushed her backside, "Vikram is in Bangalore for an official trip and Monica and children are spending the weekend at the Dulla's farmhouse. The coast is clear. Keep the door opened an inch or two and switch off the light. We should keep an eye out for the servants," she instructed Sid.

"We? I am not part of this fiasco!"

"Keep it down!" she advised and turned back to the clothes, opening and shutting drawers.

"Where is the underwear section?" She spoke to herself, looking through her daughter-in-law's closet.

"Why do you want to rummage into someone's underwear?" Sid's asked curiously, stepping into the room and standing over his mother.

Tina looked up at her son, from where she was squatting, and laughed up at him. She had been feeling around at the back of Monica's delicates section and she pulled out a small white bottle.

Tina shook her head at him, "My dear son, people hide things in this cabinet most often. They subconsciously think that owing to the private nature of the…ah…garments placed here, people won't look through them."

She giggled again sheepishly, "Biji keeps Darji's pictures in there, I bet she takes them out and kisses him every night," she laughed, "Your father keeps his revolver, Vikram a big bag of chocolates and he also has some unsigned partnership deeds dated a week before your wedding," she opened a drawer in the neighbouring cupboard and displayed the mound of sweets kept hidden under his pristine white briefs, "Yuvi is a strange one, I couldn't find anything stashed in his cupboard, just some crepe bandages and his delicates. I bet he has a locker in a bank to hide his stuff, that shrewd boy," she shook her head at that and then added wickedly, "and you hide your ah...special magazines in yours, don't you?"

"Mom! You have been poking around in my room as well?" Sid decided to take refuge in his anger to help hide his embarrassment.

Tina laughed outright at seeing him blush, "Don't worry, honey. I didn't go through them all in detail," she teased.

Sid exhaled loudly and changing the subject of his discomfiture slid down next to his mother on the floor.

"You've been searching everyone's room?" he asked interested.

"I have been playing detective," she replied breezily.

"What you are doing is dangerous." When Tina didn't respond Sid added, "The murderer won't shy away from striking twice."

Tina waved away this caution and instead displayed the bottle she had unearthed from Monica's drawer with evident delight, "Look what your mom has found!"

"A medicine bottle?"

"Monica has hidden some medicine in her lingerie drawer when she can keep it in the perfectly spacey medicine cabinet in the bathroom. Why?" she stressed.

"She doesn't want anyone else to find it," Sid stated the obvious in a bored voice.

"*Why?*" she asked, standing up and facing Sid. Her voice became firm and her eyes were lucid with all traces of mirth evaporating from them.

Sid looked at her with respect as her meaning dawned on him. He knew that his mother was frivolous and infuriating but she had grasped this situation quite rightly.

Sid took the bottle from her and looked it over, "These are sleeping pills."

"Some were used in your milk, on your wedding night. Remember?"

Looking at it intently, he spoke very slowly, as if to himself, "Monica may be taking these pills herself."

"Then why not keep the bottle in the medicine closet?" Tina asked, snatching the bottle from her son's grasp.

"You mean to say, she killed Gulab?" Sid asked, perplexed.

"Of course not!" she frowned at Sid, "Upma is the murderess," she turned the bottle in her hand and said thoughtfully, "I have yet to understand the true significance of this clue."

He heard the sound of footsteps in the corridor. Instantly on alert, he shushed her with a finger on his lips indicating the sounds outside. Both listened intently to the footsteps getting louder by the second. The sounds of feet were followed by Monica's nasal voice and Sid's heart drummed at the thought of being found out. Cornered, Tina looked from side to side and opening the door of the connecting children's room rushed into it, pulling along Sid and closing the door silently after them.

She hunkered near the keyhole with her ear pressed to it and indicated Sid to follow suit. As if they were already not in enough trouble, Sid thought. He was about to dash out the other door into the corridor but thinking it a possibility that someone was still in the corridor, he sat down on a small chair near his mother till the coast was clear.

"Why are the lights on in my room?"

Tina popped her eye to the keyhole. Dressed in blue jeans and a pink top, the tall lanky frame of Monica came in sight.

"Maybe you forgot to put the lights off in the first place, just like you forgot your weekend bag," Sara's voice was dripping with sarcasm.

"I forgot, so what?"

Ned replied sternly, "You know how we hate coming here these days. You could have been more careful, Monica."

"You could have stayed in the car while I got it," Monica replied caustically.

"And give these Mehtas something else to talk about."

"They are afraid to come in, they are guilty," he mimicked KD's rich authoritative voice.

"Guilty! Gulab was bad lot. Sara did well by killing her."

In the other room, Sid was instantly on alert. He immediately joined his mother on the floor to listen attentively through the keyhole.

"I didn't kill her!" Sara said for the umpteenth time in her defence.

"I just meant we won't blame you if you did kill her, my dear," Monica said placating. "After all, that girl deserved it" Monica soothed her sister.

"You should know Sara better than that!" Ned's voice was harsh. "Why would Sara kill Gulab?" Ned asked perplexedly.

Monica couldn't meet his eyes and prevaricated by saying:

"The humiliation and pain she put you guys through! She was bad lot!" Monica repeated.

Sara asked adamantly, "Monica, do you really think I am that monstrous? Even if she did steal my love, could I actually kill her for that?"

"I know! I know!" Monica's voice was ripe with indecision. "I just want you to know that even if you did kill her, I don't think any less of you. I am your elder sister, the only family you have, I will support you and Ned any which ways. You guys can trust me and come clean with me," her voice was earnest and she looked at them solemnly.

"There you go again!" Ned was getting angrier by the minute. He lit up a cigarette to stop himself from shaking his sister, till she dropped her fixation of blaming Sara for Gulab's murder.

Monica dropped down on her bed and rubbed her hands with vacillation. Finally, coming to a decision, her body slouched in defeat, she blurted out in a hurry before she could change her mind:

"I *know* Sara did it!," she exclaimed, "I picked up her hair from Sid's bed when I went to wake him up after we found Gulab's body. It was a small red hair on the pristine white pillow meant for Gulab. What was your hair doing on their conjugal bed?" she asked with force.

Tina gulped in the children's room and the bottle of pills dropped from her hand. She hastily picked it up and looked at Sid guiltily. For a moment Sid thought that they were about to be caught but the heat in the other room masked all the outside noises from the occupants mind. Sid heaved a sigh of relief and applied his ear once more to the keyhole.

"I never went near that bed!" Sara exclaimed with genuine surprise. "That hair can't be mine."

"All of us sat on the sofa for a few minutes that night and that's too far away from the bed," Ned added slowly.

"Unless the bearer of the hair went in once again inside the room," Monica sighed.

"Where is it? The hair?" asked Ned.

Monica said acerbically, "I threw it out the window. Where else will it be? Hidden in my purse?"

"We could have got it tested for DNA had you had the good sense to keep it hidden in your purse," Ned threw back at her.

Monica had the grace to look ashamed upon hearing the rebuke.

"May I ask why you assumed that hair to be Sara's?"

"It was red! Have you not been listening to me?"

"But so is mine," he stressed, "Why does it have to be Sara's?" He looked directly into Monica's eyes, his stare glacial.

"Why would you be on Sid's bed?" Monica said with meaning.

"Why would Sara be?" Ned asked undeterred.

Monica averted her face.

"Answer me!" Ned's chest heaved with anger.

Monica blushed but she supplied nonetheless:

"Sid and she were engaged once."

"So? They *were* and Sid is someone else's husband *now*." Ned was reproachful.

"Maybe that is the whole problem," Monica said harshly.

"Stop it both of you!" Sara intervened in a tough but hushed voice, "you want us to be overheard?!" she fumed.

The leashed anger in Sara's voice managed to pacify the

heated argument. Monica offered a tardy apology:

"Okay. So, I assumed wrong and it wasn't Sara's hair. But no one else has red hair in our family let alone the vibrant red you two have. And I had personally taken care of the decoration of the wedding bed. The white sheet and pillows were spotless, without a speck of dust let alone a hair. It came there from someone's head. I am convinced," she said priggishly.

"We didn't even go near the bed that night." Ned said assertively.

"I have an idea," Monica stood up and faced her siblings. "The effect of poison Gulab was given is instantaneous, isn't it Sara?" After receiving a small nod from Sara, Monica continued:

"It means she was poisoned after we left her alone with Sid," her eyes gleamed, "It means, Sid could have murdered her and then planted the evidence including the hair to make it seem that Sara came back to the room. But as fate would have it I got hold of the hair and destroyed it." Monica concluded triumphantly.

In the other room, Sid sucked in a deep breath. His mother patted his shoulder and silently prodded him to keep listening.

"That's a good point." Ned conceded.

"Someone *is* trying to frame me," Sara nodded, "I definitely remember removing my ear-rings and other jewels before sleeping. I kept them on the mantel piece. Did my ear-ring walk to the Pavilion?!

"And talking about my jewels, did you find my ring?" Sara asked her sister. "It was a princess cut 3.25 carat solitaire and is missing since the night of the murder."

Monica shook her head in negation, "I have asked everyone here but it's nowhere to be found."

"Then my ring also has feet!"

"I think, whoever took the earring also took Sara's ring, to frame her, but for some reason didn't use it. We find the ring and it will lead us to the killer," Ned gasped excitedly.

"Brilliant suggestion," Sara looked at her brother with awe.

"Why don't we surreptitiously check everyone's room for the ring?" Sara suggested.

"Yes, after the weekend when no one would be home."

Both Sara and Ned nodded in agreement.

"Now that we are so close to finding out the murderer, I don't want any of the family members to be the culprit," Monica sighed sadly, picking up the weekend bag they had come to collect. "After all they are my family. It would be best if Mom is right and our maid Upma did it."

"Does she have some proof?" Ned asked.

"No, just an intuitive guess," Monica added, "But we do know something which others don't. Do you think....?"

Sara cut her off before she could finish the sentence.

"No! We are already in enough trouble," she said with heat in her voice.

"Sara is right. Let's just stick to our original statements. That's for the best."

"Moreover, it won't solve any purpose. Upma didn't have any motive to kill Gulab but all three of us had. In fact if looks could kill, Gulab would have been dead long ago," Ned smiled sadly.

Saying this Ned took the travel bag from Monica's hand and all three of them left the room leaving behind two huddled eavesdroppers agreeing with Ned's last statement. The shadow of the swaying trees on the walls filled Sid's mind with sinister thoughts. The Dullas won't be given the opportunity to find that ring, he swore. It was time to roll out his plan.

Finally it Happened

*T*he air had been filled with hope that spring; it had smelled of sweet sweat, not only of the Indian Cricket team which had managed to reach the finals by defeating their arch rivals, Pakistan, but of all the Indians who were playing in their gardens, on roads or even in their living rooms, consumed by the cricket fever. It had been World Cup time once again and all the cricket lovers in Mumbai, where I was living for the past few months, were gearing up to cheer India while we took the trophy home.

Except me. I had different plans for that day.

Sid loved cricket and I wanted to be there with him for the World Cup finals so I planned a small surprise trip to Ratnagiri. I reached Ratnagiri around six in the evening and was off to the palace in a jiffy. Unfortunately Sid was not home, the maid informed me. His cell phone was also switched off. I guessed he would be enjoying the match with his friends, squatting at one of their places. In a spur of brilliance I called Yuvi.

"Gulab!" Yuvraj's voice was filled with delight. We talked everyday on phone since I shifted to Mumbai and it was evident in our conversations that Yuvi missed me sorely. He had completed a course in Hospitality Management and was doing his internship under his father's guidance.

"Do you know where Sid is?" I asked.

He spoke a moment too late than he should have and some of the excitement ebbed from his voice.

"No," Yuvi replied.

"I am outside your home. I came specifically from Mumbai to catch this match with Sid...." I sounded depressed and tired.

" I'll be with you in five minutes flat!" He sounded way too excited. He rarely expressed such intense emotions and I couldn't help but smile at his childish delight at the prospect of meeting me.

"But Yuvi, you don't want to miss the match," I protested.

" I'll catch the highlights later," he replied. In a decibel lower than his earlier excited tone he added, "I can help you find Sid faster."

Exactly five minutes later Yuvi pulled up his Harley near my car. He engulfed me in a warm bear hug, his ponytail ticked my nose and I tried to push him away laughingly.

"Yuvi, your pony is up to its dirty tricks," I reprimanded jokingly.

"How I have missed you, Gulab!" He breathed into my hair. As if coming to himself, he instantly pulled away and starting his bike said breezily, "Hop on, Princess. Let's find your prince charming."

He took me to a couple of Sports bars where Sid's friends were hanging out but we were unable to trace him. It was getting late and my urgency to find Sid knew no bounds. At last Yuvi turned the bike out of the town.

"Yuvi, where are we heading?" I asked looking around the hilly terrain.

"Ned's place," he replied.

"Ned... Monica's brother, right? The one from London?"

My voice was drifting with the cool mountainous breeze and I shouted over Yuvi's shoulder to be heard.

"Yes."

"I never really met him at the wedding."

"Sid has been hanging with Dullas quite a bit. Let's check him out there."

Yuvi parked the bike outside a farmhouse and asked me to wait there for him. He returned a few minutes later.

Without Sid.

My face fell and heart sank. My last hope was dashed.

To Yuvi I looked like a beautiful mermaid who was forced to live on land but who ached to be back in water. He didn't like the idea of Sid being the water I so wanted to be in. His eyes hardened and against his better judgment he said:

"I have found Sid."

"You are a saviour!" my pulse quickened at the prospect of finally meeting Sid.

In no time Yuvi drove us to a famous French restaurant in the heart of Ratnagiri.

"OMG! This place had a romantic candlelit ambiance with subtle piano music in the background. How come they opened it to loud beer drinking sports enthusiasts?" I shook my head and envisioned the power of cricket in our country.

I started running towards the entrance. Strangely no loud noise was penetrating the walls and reaching me. I was disappointed to think that the match had ended and worse still we had lost to the Lankans.

" I think we lost the match," I looked around, but to my surprise Yuvi wasn't with me. I turned and saw him standing near his bike. He signalled me to go on without him.

Paying no heed to the immaculately dressed hostess I rushed into the dining area. It took me a while to acclimatize to the subtle lighting. My eyes dashed everywhere at once. There were no more than ten people in an otherwise fully reserved establishment and it was not the venue for screening the match.

The tinkling of her soft laughter drew me towards them. She had her back to me and opposite her sitting holding her hands, as debonair as ever, was my Sid.

Before my eyes, my world crumbled into tiny bits and pieces. Sid bent on his one knee still holding her hands and in his honey suckled voice said those three words which he had repeated to me thousands of times.

"I love you," he breathed.

My heart squashed. I was routed to the spot looking at the spectacle of his love for someone else.

"Ma'am, a table for two perhaps?" The waiter's umpteenth enquiry got to me at last and shook me out of my stupor. I looked at him as if he were a spectre and without looking back at Sid, left the restaurant.

The night welcomed me once again and I kept on walking into its darkness. Away from Sid. A familiar voice called after me. I didn't care. I didn't stop. Suddenly Yuvi was beside me. He held my arms and shook me hard.

"Where are you going?"

My diluted vision focused once more on the reality. The rhythmic hum of traffic finally managed to reach me and I realized that I was walking in the middle of a crowded noisy road. There were horns beaming crankily around me. Yuvi pulled me onto the pavement and hugged me tenderly.

"I know about Sid and Sara. I am sorry, Gulab. But I couldn't shield you from the reality for long. It wasn't fair to you," he said

in a brittle voice.

"Don't worry, I am fine," I said in a dead voice.

Suddenly the sky went ablaze with fireworks. The voice of cheering, clapping and laughter reached me from everywhere.

"We won," Yuvi sighed.

The whole city seemed to be on the road, dancing with merriment. The tri coloured flags waving at me from afar, the shrieks of joy, the whistles filled with excitement or the animated cheering of the exuberant crowd did nothing for my clogged emotions. My eyes were curiously empty. I didn't cry that day or any other day after that. Except for that lonesome tear which managed to escape my eyes on my last night in this world.

A weight had finally lifted off my chest. The torture of waiting for the dreaded had finally ended. There was an ounce of relief mixed with my pain.

The Ghost in White

Sid was restlessly walking the grounds of the Royal Hill when a bout of heavy rain made him rush to the back patio. He sat there wringing his hands agitatedly, waiting for the phone call he was expecting any minute now. It had the power to either pull him out of his troubles or conversely push him into a deep abyss of problems. Who could have thought that Gulab's death would open this can of worms for him, he sighed anxiously.

A pat on his arm from behind made him look over his shoulder. The old gardener's shrewd eyes were appraising him. Handing him a dry towel the gardener said quietly:

"Baba, dry yourself before you catch cold."

"Thank you, kaka."

Sid accepted the proffered towel and turned his head back towards the rain, signalling the end of the dialogue.

Malviya *kaka* cleared his throat. A slightly embarrassed intonation made itself heard in his voice as he said:

"No matter how much faith we have, we often lose people. But we never forget them. And sometimes, it's these memories that give us the power to go on. Make them your strength not weakness."

"I just wish I could roll back the clocks….," as if coming to himself Sid glanced sideways at his old servant.

The gardener sighed. "We can't change destiny."

"I'm holding on to something that used to be there hoping it will come back…." Sid's words were thoughtful.

"Come back? But she hasn't gone anywhere, Baba."

Sid looked hard at his companion.

"I know how everyone says that people stay alive in our memories. But I want her with me, here, not in some fictional memory world. She has gone away from me, *Kaka*. "

The old man looked at Sid rather oddly and said:

"But Memsaab is still in the palace!"

Sid's eyebrows drew together in surprise and he spluttered:

"*Kaka,* have you been drinking?! My wife died and I don't appreciate such un-thoughtful remarks about her."

The old man drew himself up and said:

"I don't drink."

He paused and then said unexpectedly, "I know she is no more alive, Baba. But she hasn't yet left this world. I have seen her with my own two eyes."

Sid said bluntly:

"You are an old man. Your eyes are weak. And I think you have lost your mind on top of that!"

The gardener crouched on his hinges and said with more spontaneity than he had yet shown, "I saw her on your balcony on the morning after her murder. She was dressed in a white robe and it was blowing in the air. Her back was towards me but it was Memsaab alright! "

Sid turned the idea over in his mind, "You may have mistaken Monica's or Mom's balcony for mine."

"How can I? Servant quarters are just next to the lake, near the Pavilion. Just like from the Pavilion we can see only two rooms. Yours and Yuvi baba's. I definitely saw her on your balcony."

Sid asked incredulously, "At what time?"

"Just after I woke up at 4:30 am. I was going to take a bath and happened to see the lights from my window. The decorative lighting for the wedding looked so pretty. I stood admiring it when I happened to see her. I remember asking myself what Memsaab was doing standing there all alone. When I came back from the bathroom she was no longer there."

"She wasn't even alive at 4:30 am. Are you sure that it was my balcony?"

"I am sure, Baba. I may be an old ignorant fool but I am no liar." After a pause he continued, "She is still around wanting to contact you...."

Saying this he smiled sympathetically and went away, hunched and old.

Sid sat staring into the distance for some time. A new thought had taken shape in his head. A recently overheard conversation kept nagging at the back of his mind. What had Monica said about the red hair on his bed? She had believed it to be Sara's. With Kaka witnessing a lady on his balcony it definitely pointed towards Sara. Sid's milk was found to be drugged so obviously he couldn't have seen her coming or going. The police will have a field day with this idea, he sighed contentedly. It was one more proof against Sara, he cheered himself. She could have been on his balcony erasing proofs and the old gardener would see the truth of the situation with a little prodding, he was sure. The gardener would testify against Sara, Sid nodded with satisfaction.

His lips curved, at the thought of luck finally being on his side. His being a suspect was definitely bothering him a lot not to mention the creditor's threats and Vikram's ultimatum. But this statement from *Kaka* would clench the whole investigation against Sara, he smiled. For the first time he was hopeful that within the seven days left for the police to submit the report, he would be able to build up a strong case against Sara and in turn acquire his freedom and peace of mind once again.

He just had to wait for that phone call now, he sighed with mild irritation.

A Career Girl

I returned to Ratnagiri exactly a year after that disastrous World Cup match. I had left for good that same night. Yuvi tried to contact me for months on end but I never responded. I got a few calls from Sid as well but didn't exchange as much as a message with him. I just changed my cell number and gave instructions at my father's house to not share it with anyone from the palace. Yuvi managed to get it somehow though, but I had vowed to sever all ties with the Mehtas and if it meant sacrificing my only true friend, Yuvi, this new remorseless Gulab didn't give two hoots. Yuvi came to Mumbai a few weeks later but I didn't meet him. He eventually gave in but called often just waiting for me to reject his call. It was as if that was all the communication he desired. Needless to say, knowing that he was there for me gave me a great deal of emotional support in those gloomy weeks.

My broken heart coupled with the culture of Mumbai, which I readily accepted after my return, had an effect on my overall personality. The drive to build an enviable career took the place of my earlier passion for love. When I left Salandale, I had an apprenticeship with an international bank in my one hand and a radically different personality in the other. I was much slender now and proficiently enhanced my features using make up. I still wore Punjabi suits but these were the creations of the best Indian *designers, stylish and modern. I discarded my imitation jewellery and instead wore diamonds, rubies and pearls. I had come to Salandale as an uncertain teenager but had matured to be a confident and self assured young lady at the time of leaving.*

My job in Mumbai was my life now. When my father sent a message to visit him I was quite surprised. In the time I had been in Mumbai he had never revealed a desire for me to visit Ratnagiri. Knowing my father, I guessed this to be one of our meetings in which he ordered a decree to be followed, most likely something to do with his political campaign. A solid family front was always welcomed by the public and in such scenarios I was used as a pawn, a dutiful loving daughter.

Whatever his reasons for wanting to meet me, I decided to go back one last time to the town that haunted my memories.

The Heart Saw All

The faint chirping of the sparrows drew Ned to the back porch. His peaceful surroundings offered him the desperately needed dose of tranquillity, what with the upheaval created by the police officials at his residence. Earlier in the day a team of cops had come barging into his home, fully armed with a search warrant. They had sealed the house and Sara's laboratory. Both Sara and he were not allowed to communicate till the search was in progress. Sara was confined to the lab and Ned was forced to while away his time in the house. He silently thanked God for having sent the children to the playground with Monica earlier in the day.

What the police expected to find was beyond Ned. They definitely couldn't unearth their secret by undertaking some petty search. Their tracks were well covered. This process was just a formality and fretting about it was uncalled for, Ned placated himself.

A little more relaxed, he perched on the swing hanging from a tree and closed his eyes. The to and fro motion of the swing and the gentle breeze slapping him playfully drew him into a slumber. Within a few minutes he was pulled into the web of the same dream which had been haunting him with its vividness for days. This time she was wearing red, the same shade that she had been wearing the day they had first met.

"My Rose!" He breathed.

As always, she had her back to him. Her red skirts flowing around her, she was moving away from him. As expected, suddenly she turned. He was drawn to her eyes once more. But strangely they were not the hazel colour he knew them to be. They were grey, clear and transparent. Just like his. He was impishly delighted by this change. This colour matched her personality much better.

He called out to her, "Rose!"

She smiled at him and started gliding towards him. There was an edge to her today, which made her look much more beautiful than usual. Her wispy red dress with a plunging neckline slithered on her like it always did. Her shining eyes the only jewels adorning her body. But he felt quite potently something to be different today. He couldn't dispel this notion and try as he might he couldn't put a finger to it.

Reaching him, she held the ropes of the swing on either side of him and moved closer, bangles clinking. She bent to look into his eyes. The wind blew her hair away from her face and Ned got a whiff of her perfume as she touched her lips lightly to his ear yet again. The dream always burst into reality at this stage and Ned prayed ardently for her to speak before he woke up.

"Ned," she whispered. She asked in her singularly sweet voice, soft and clear. "You liked my gift?"

A bird screeched and Ned was mercilessly pulled out of the dream. He looked around frantically for her, knowing full well that she had not been real. The experience left him disconcerted. It coerced him to dive in for those suppressed memories he had locked away, months back and had thrown the key into a deep sea for fear that he might retrieve it one day. That had been the only way to keep sane. But the lock was now opened and memories started spilling towards him.

Gulab, she had certainly been dressed like her namesake, the first time he saw her. In a white salwaar suit, he could still recall, and a red bandhani dupatta hugging her body pristinely. Her curls were rebelliously escaping the bun at the nape of her neck and she was continuously fiddling to tuck them back in, Ned smiled reminiscently. Her heart-shaped face was devoid of any make up except her big hazel eyes darkly lined with kohl and her lips matching her dupatta, more crimson than red. Her appearance somehow made her seem untamed, wild.

As he entered the establishment, he saw her sitting alone in a corner in the candle lit ambiance of 'The Pit's Bistro'. She had looked so forlorn staring into the space that he had wanted to reach out and comfort her. He deliberately took a seat from where he could surreptitiously glance in her direction.

They were a group of ten people including Sid, Monica, Sara and a few other friends. She didn't look towards them, lost in her own world.

"Gulab!" Sid's surprised voice forced her out of her reverie.

She looked in their direction wide eyed and dropped her spoon. It fell into the bowl and splattered the soup she had been trying to eat. Her face paled as if the ghosts of her dreams had suddenly become real. She regained her poise in a minute and smiled politely in their direction.

Ned's eyes had hardened. He looked at Sara and their eyes met. He could see the dismay in her eyes as she witnessed the way Sid was looking approvingly in Gulab's direction. Sara's jealousy was so intense that it was palpable. Whenever one of them experienced extreme emotions the other could feel it like their own. Sid had broken up with Gulab but very often her name crept up in the conversations un-beckoned and Sid's eyes lit up. Even Ned noticed the hold Gulab still had on him and resented it as much as his sister.

After a few minutes Gulab paid her bill and left the table.

Ned had covertly followed her out. She was about to drive off when he knocked on the window of the driver's seat.

She had lowered it and asked, "Yes?"

"Stay away from Sid," Ned had ordered.

He could never forget her face, as he saw it then; it had been etched into his memory. Her features were outlined against the bright light from the street lamps. Her head was tilted to one side and her eyes were blinking at him, appraising him. Those remarkable hazel eyes, green highlighted with gold, different from any other woman's that he had ever known.

Gulab had asked incredulously, "And who are you?"

"I am Sara's brother," he had replied.

"Ah! We never met at Monica's wedding," she replied amicably after placing him.

"I don't want to chit chat. Just stay away from my sister's boyfriend. If anyone tries to hurt her, he or she will have to deal with me first. And let me tell you that I am a very bad enemy," Ned had said in a threatening voice.

Gulab had burst into peals of laughter upon hearing his threat. Ned looked at her and his stern features melted. Ned had a sudden feeling that this girl didn't laugh much.

When the fit of laughter subsided, she said softly, "Assuming that I wish to rekindle old flames, what makes you think that Sid would be interested in anyone other than your sister?"

Ned couldn't meet her eyes and she didn't persist for a reply. "I have experienced quite a life with Sid and I truly hope that your sister has managed to change him." Looking into the distance she spoke softly, "I haven't talked to Sid for the past one year. And I don't intend to for the rest of my life,"

She asked with a smile, her gaze once again directed at Ned, "I hope that satisfies you?"

She started closing the window of the car but stopped when Ned asked, "What if he comes back to you?"

Looking straight into his eyes, she replied, "If he comes back to me, you should probably question your sister. Whether she wants to be with such a fickle man?"

"Will you take him back?" Ned had persisted.

"Can you keep a secret?"

Ned had been surprised by the question but he nodded in assent.

"I am getting married."

At that moment Ned had felt a stone being lifted from his heart and a new, heavier and bulkier one being placed instead. It was a strange feeling.

He said automatically, "Congratulations."

"I won't come in your sister's way. Trust me."

And Ned had trusted her from that day on. His family believed that she had betrayed him but his heart knew better. Sometimes the heart sees what is invisible to the eye. He didn't know why she did what she did but somehow he still trusted her, despite his actions.

The loud voices of the police officials coming towards him brought him back to the present. He got up from the swing and met them halfway.

Inspector Sharma said in a formal voice: "We would need to take your sister with us for questioning."

"She has already answered all your questions, Inspector," Ned frowned.

"Some new evidence has come to light," he replied mysteriously.

"New evidence?" Ned repeated, confused.

"Your sister had potassium cyanide in her laboratory as per records. We can't find that vial in her lab now. We think that the poison used on Gulab was taken from here."

Ned saw Sara coming out with a few officials and their eyes met. There was panic in her eyes and confusion in his.

"I don't know how that vial went missing," she cried. "I haven't even touched it for months."

From behind Ned, Sid and KD came into view, their expressions triumphant. They had been silently waiting near the police jeep for quite some time.

Sid's voice was acidic, "Inspector, this girl murdered my wife. I want her behind bars."

"Please come with us, Ma'am," the officials prodded Sara to move towards their jeep.

"I didn't kill Gulab. Please believe me, Inspector," she implored. "The vial has been stolen from my lab, to implicate me."

"No one is saying that you are a murderer, Sara," Ned looked pointedly at Sid, their eyes duelling. "The inspector just wants to ask a few questions. That's all." Ned touched Sara's shoulder, trying to calm her down. When her eyes still remained panic stricken, Ned cupped her cheeks and looked deep into her eyes. "Don't you trust your brother? Humn?"

After a few seconds, Sara nodded, a little of her inherent calm restored.

"I'll drive Sara to the police station, if you don't mind," before the inspector could oppose, he shrugged, "Or would you rather get a warrant?"

"Ma'am can drive with you," the inspector conceded, albeit reluctantly.

As Ned crossed Sid, their eyes clashed. "I challenge you to save Sara. I won't rest until she rots in the jail," Sid spoke through clenched teeth.

"And I won't rest until my sister is proven innocent. I swear to you!" Ned's eyes were filled with rage.

"From now on you and your family are not welcome to the palace. Stay away from us," Sid added with force.

"What did you just say? *My* family is not welcome in *my* home?" Monica spoke headedly. She had been listening to their conversation from afar, the twins on either side of her.

"Anyone whose sympathies are with Gulab's murderer is not welcome in *my* home. Including you." KD ordered, before moving to his car, "Stay here until this investigation ends."

As Sid followed his father, his eyes twinkled with victory. The police have finally found their murderer in Sara, he sighed, and the report will highlight the same leaving Sid free of all his worries. His gamble had paid off, he exhaled with relief. And with cunning he had even contrived to keep the Dullas away from the palace. Now how will they search the palace for the ring? With only six days left to submit the report, how would Ned save his darling sister? His lips curved in a sinister smile.

But had he known what was brewing up in Ned's mind, his smile would have faded in no time.

A Whisper on my Pillow

I

*M*y *work in Ratnagiri done, I took the first flight out. Accepting my father's terms was not a compulsion for me, I simply didn't want to refuse. And by doing so I had managed to acquire not only the respect of my family members but also an ounce of my father's love.*

I was casually flipping through a magazine when someone called my name.

It was Ned. Dressed formally in a one button grey pin stripped suit, he looked suave. He smiled at me and its candidness charmed me. Pointing at the empty seat next to him, he signalled me to join him. I was trying to think of a polite way to refuse but he mouthed:

"Please!"

I gave in and changed my seat. The pungent smell of smoke invaded my nostrils. Ned was a chain smoker, I had guessed rightly.

He casually stroked his short and spiky hair. "I called for you at your home and was told you had already left for the airport to fly back to Mumbai. I followed you here."

I asked laughingly, "To the airplane?!"

"Church bells!"

"What?"

"Your laughter. It's like church bells," he smiled, taking a deep breath and closing his eyes, *"Pristine."*

"Thanks," I said self consciously. Compliments disconcerted me and I changed the topic of our conversation. *"Why did you follow me?"*

"I wanted to apologize for my behaviour yesterday," he shook his head repentantly. *"I am sorry. I got carried away."*

He didn't seem like a man who needed to apologize a lot. But he did it with grace and it was heartfelt.

"It's natural for you to be protective of your sister," I said with a small smile.

'Why are you so charitable about Sara?"

"What do you mean?" I frowned.

"She took Sid away from you."

"Had he been mine, Sara couldn't have taken him away," I sighed. *"Ah….She knew we were still together, when..uh…?"* I asked hesitatingly.

"Yes."

Both of us were quiet for some time.

He asked after a minute, *"Are you less charitable now?"*

I shook my head.

He looked straight into my eyes and said, *"You are just as beautiful inside."*

He replied to my questioning look:

"You look stunning. Hasn't anyone ever told you?"

I blushed under his appreciative gaze and looked away. He burst out in peals of laughter.

"But I definitely like you better in the Punjabi suit you were wearing yesterday and your casually coiled hair bun. That wild look is the real you." He crinkled his nose at my cream formal

trousers, crisp black shirt and gelled hair, "That's so not you."

"Rose," he smiled, "This name suits you much better than the demure Gulab."

He was the first guy who had complimented me for my rustic dressing sense. The resident weird girl of Ratnagiri was not used to that. I looked at him sternly and said in a crisp voice, "I don't like flirts."

The air hostess came with our breakfast and both of us ate in silence. After our tray had been cleared Ned sensed an improvement in my mood. He ventured a hand at conversation once again.

"You are still studying?"

I explained about my internship in Mumbai. Without looking at me, he asked:

"Your fiancé is in Mumbai?"

I don't know why I told him but I couldn't stop myself from saying, "I don't know where he lives."

"You don't want to tell?"

"I don't know his name, qualifications or address," I put it clearly in words.

He looked at me as if I had lost my mind.

"It's an arranged marriage," I clarified succinctly.

His expression didn't alter and I had an outlandish urge to tell him all.

"It is a political union. My father has arranged it," I added.

"You don't know him?!" He exclaimed.

"I didn't want to know." I replied carelessly.

"You will spend the rest of your life with him!"

I shrugged offhandedly.

"You don't mind this business arrangement cum marriage?"his

voice vibrated angrily.

"This is just a favour to my father. The first one he has ever asked of me," I looked away so that he couldn't peek at the pain hidden in my eyes. "He needs some big money for the coming elections and his industrialist friend needs the political clout. This marriage will do the trick," I replied simply.

"But what about you?" he asked exasperated.

"I don't believe in fairytales anymore. This marriage is quite practical. I'll be back at my job within a month and I'll divorce this guy in a few years time. Once the charade is over I'll be free to pursue my life the way I want," I smiled uneasily.

"You are free to follow your heart even now. Why this wedding?" It was half a question and half a plea.

"This is a gift for my father," I closed my eyes and pictured him once again asking me for getting into this loveless marriage. I had seen his eyes shining with pride at me being his daughter, for the first time in my life, when I had accepted his offer in front of his whole family. He had hugged me in pleasure, again a first for me. I had eventually proved my worth to him even if it meant sacrificing a few years of my life in a sham marriage.

"How can he use you like this! If someone tried to do this to Sara, I'll kill him!" his voice was harsh and his facial expression mirrored his feelings.

"Both of you are very close," I observed with envy.

"We are twins. We share the warm comfort that comes from having someone understand our deepest thoughts and feelings."

"She is lucky."

"Both of us are. She can read me like an open book too," he smiled and added, "She is my life. I would prefer to die before seeing her in pain."

The airhostess announced asking us to fasten our seat belts and prepare for the landing.

As we moved to collect our baggage I said awkwardly, biting my lip:

"I don't know why I shared my uh… marriage details with you. Can you please keep it to yourself?"I added, "I don't want it to reach Mehtas."

We were walking but he stopped midway and held my hand. Gazing into my eyes he promised, "It's a secret between us. Trust me. Just like I trusted you."

The way he said it conjured up a long forgotten image of my mother. The pledge in his voice rang as true as used to be in hers. I just nodded, pulled my hand away from his grasp and started moving again.

"Rose," he called after me by a name he had christened me.

I turned to look back at him.

He said, "I have to be back in Ratnagiri for a lunch meeting."

"You came all the way to Mumbai to go back by the next flight!"

"I came all the way to Mumbai to apologize to you. I was way out of line. And so was Sara when she dated Sid while he was still bound to you. Forgive us."

I nodded once again and said graciously but with a heavy heart for an apology couldn't get me my life back. "No hard feelings."

Saying this I walked away.

II

I had walked away from Ned, from Yuvi, from Ratnagiri and from my dreams. But walking away from my conscience was not that easy. The enormity of my decision to marry a stranger to buy off my father's respect started sinking in. These were not my values, I gulped. I had reduced the pious institution of marriage into a demeaning business association.

I was drowning my ethics in wine. It had helped me in the past year to smother my sorrows and I hoped it would rid me of that tickle which pronounced sixty times in a minute that I was sinking in the eyes of my dead mother. A bottle down and my inebriated self still continued to reprimand me. How could I make a joke out of a sacred relationship?

Staggering towards the window I peeked at the night sky from the confines of my room. I had asked the stars in the sky repeatedly in my drunken state:

"Is this my destiny, this make-believe marriage? Tell me...tell me..."

A knock on the door seemed like destiny wanting me to open a new door. I swayed forth and embraced my fate.

"I can't marry without love. I can't. Tell me I don't have to!" I shouted in my drunken stupor and clutched at him. He didn't let me go. Closing the door after him he guided me towards the couch and laid me gently there. Along with my scruples my insides also burst forth and I splattered the carpeted floor with my puke. The wine couldn't swallow my conscience but it drew me into the world of dreams. I imagined a wet towel touching my face. I snuggled deeper into the couch and went back to sleep.

I dreamed of a man crouching on the floor, cleaning it and after some time the stink of my reeking was replaced by the fragrance of flowers. I inhaled it again and again. I could also inhale a warm musky smell, cigarette smoke. I sniffed again and slid closer to the smell. Someone was sitting next to me and smoking. I tilted my head and placed it on a strong thigh. After a while strong hands picked me up and settled me comfortably into my bed. They pulled a sheet over me and patting my cheek said in a very soft reassuring voice:

"You won't have to marry without love. I promise."

The voice was so comforting that the throbbing in my head instantly seized and I said with confidence, "I trust you."

Before sleep could finally engulf me a ghost of a smile touched my lips and I muttered, "Smoking kills."

A feather light laugh touched my ear, "So does drinking."

I buried my face in my pillows and was comatose in an undisturbed slumber.

I woke up to the smell of coffee and for a baffled moment wondered who could be in my apartment. I couldn't remember letting anyone in. I could recall drinking wine. My memory instantly returned at this thought. Clutching my throbbing head, I rushed out into the living room and to my utter surprise saw Ned standing in the kitchen, fluffing an omelette. I rubbed my eyes hurriedly to clear my vision. It couldn't be Ned, I thought. He didn't know where I lived.

He smiled at me and asked politely, "Hangover?"

"What are you doing here?" I strutted towards him.

He brought forth two steaming cups of coffee and handed me one.

"Making coffee."

I was irked at him for being so comfortable in my home.

"Why are you here?" I asked angrily, thumping the cup down on the kitchen table, spilling coffee over the brim.

"You didn't seem to have any problems about that last night. Even welcomed me with open arms," he teased gently.

I reddened as bits and pieces of my memory started returning. "I was drunk."

"You could have fooled me," He said with a mischievous smile. It was infectious and my lips twitched a little.

Realizing that browbeating him for an answer would not work, I took a chair and started sipping my coffee.

"Omelet?" he asked.

"No thanks. Coffee is fine," I answered. I added sarcastically, "Help yourself to anything you like."

He pulled a chair opposite me and tucked into his omelette.

"I was famished," he said polishing off his plate in a few quick bites. Without breaking the flow of his words he put in:

"I had a talk with your father. I am funding his campaign this year and offering him a better proposition. Your so called marriage is off."

I sat open-mouthed for a few minutes on hearing it, my cup halfway to my lips. 'Should I be angry at his high handedness or relieved for getting me off the hook?' Was the first question I asked myself. A close second being- 'Why did he do this?'

When I couldn't think of anything to say, I asked sceptically, "What do you want in return?"

His warm grey eyes instantly turned icy. "Don't insult me."

"We met two days ago! Why would you do it for me?" I asked flabbergasted.

"Because I am selfish," he prevaricated.

"Is this your way of apologizing on Sara's behalf?" I asked. He sighed, "No."

He got up, dragged his chair closer to mine and said self consciously, "Rose, I like you. A lot. I want you to be my wife."

I was shocked, to say the least. I said scathingly:

"So, only the groom has changed."

The way he was looking at me reminded me of the previous night. I was smothered in my repulsive vomit and he had cleaned me gently with a wet towel. His eyes had the same expression in them today.

Affection. That's what he felt towards me. That was reflecting in his eyes.

"Rose, I am not forcing you to marry me by helping your father. I just don't want you to enter into a meaningless relation when we can have a chance at something better. I wanted to keep that door open for you and me. There is no pressure on you in terms of time you want to take to consider us or even for marrying me at all. And if you fall in love with anyone else in the meantime, you are free to have a life with him," he looked straight into my eyes and touched my hand gently. "Just give us a chance. That's all I am asking."

His offer was quite appealing but I owed it to him to be honest about my feelings. "Sid will always be in my heart. I can't forget him," I stressed, "even if I want to. You should have a partner who loves you," I tried to reason with him.

"Love has many definitions, Rose. For me love is affection. We can have a great life based on that. But you don't have to think about all that right now. Take your time."

I agree with him today, love does have many definitions.

Piecing the Clues

Sid knocked on the door of his parent's bedroom. He shifted his weight from one foot to another, and was about to pound it once again when his mother pulled it open a notch.

Tina leaned out and asked in an abrupt manner.

"What do you want?" She seemed in the throes of sleep.

"I wanted to speak to Dad."

"He is not here."

She was about to close the door on Sid's face, thought better of it and asked instead:

"Is it regarding the murder?"

Sid didn't want his mother to be a part of this discussion but considering that she wanted to get back to her beauty sleep as soon as possible, he assented. He should have known better. Sleep instantaneously vanished from her eyes and his nosy mother pulled the door fully open. She shouted:

"KD, come here. It's important."

Tina invited her son in with a casual wave of her hand.

"KD is in the boudoir with his files and papers."

"I should go there."

"As if he would listen to us with his files beckoning him

all the time!" she cribbed waving a delicate hand and asked instead:

"So you got something against Upma yet?"

Sid shook his head wearily. He was tired of his mother's fixation with the maid. Upma had been interrogated by the police and there was nothing fishy about her. His mother just wanted a scapegoat and the poor maid was an easy target. He said irritated:

"I'll go to the boudoir."

"Nonsense! Stay right here."

After a few more shouts and some violent knocks on the connecting door, KD came out in a black mood.

"Sid and I want to discuss something very important about the murder," she looked in his direction, "Sid?"

Sid raised his eyebrows and said cautiously:

"Actually, I want to discuss something in private with Dad."

Tina got up in a huff, walked to the mini bar, took out a bottle of beer and banged the door shut, before coming back to her seat. She declared:

"I am not going anywhere."

Both father and son took in her arrogant stance and without further wasting their time decided to bear with her. KD leaned back casually on the throw pillows littered on the bed and Sid pulled the sofa closer.

"I have come across something that can be used as evidence in the case. I don't want Vikram to get a scent of this. I don't trust him not to repeat it to his wife."

He looked warningly towards his mother and she shrugged her shoulders, "My lips are sealed."

"The gardener saw a woman on my balcony the night

of Gulab's death. After 4:30 a.m. He seems to thinks it was Gulab's spirit."

The beer bottle dropped from Tina's hand. She instantaneously bent to pick it up and asked surreptitiously:

"Really?"

KD spluttered:

"What crap!"

Ignoring his mother, Sid turned to his father and said excitedly:

"Consider this - he saw a woman on my balcony after Gulab had died and I was drugged!"

Sid related the whole episode with the gardener and what he and Tina had overheard in Monica's room, about the red hair.

"It was definitely the murderer or an accomplice," said KD. "But how can we prove that it was Sara? The gardener seems to think it was Gulab and we don't have that hair in our possession for getting a DNA test done."

"He says her white robe was blowing in the air, her back was to him and he couldn't see her face. He is an impressionable fellow. We'll work on him and convince him it was Sara. He will tell the police what we want."

Sid was positive in his assertions but KD shook his head.

"I don't agree with you. That man is a romantic; he won't be able to give a statement against Sara with conviction. And secondly, we may inadvertently axe ourselves by opening this line of enquiry. What if that old fool was just imagining things and no one was there on the balcony. Sara just needs to prove that she wasn't there. And if she does that the other females of our household will be open to fire once the police get it into their heads that a woman is involved," he shook his head. "It's not as easy as it seems."

Sid asked hopefully:

"The gardener says she was wearing a white gown. What if we can prove Sara was wearing white that night?"

KD scoffed.

"That old guy can't have perfect eyesight to actually see the colour of the dress from that far."

Seeing that Sid was about to protest he held up his hand to stall him and continued, "Also anyone can have a white gown. Your mother wears a white nightgown to bed. Look," he pointed in her direction, "She has one on right now."

Both father and son looked in her direction and Tina giggled nervously. "I definitely think it can be Upma in Sid's room that night. She has a white *saree*…I know….it can be confused with a robe…."

As always they ignored her and continued talking.

"I agree this is not concrete evidence but just look at the larger picture," his hands moved passionately with his words, "Firstly, Sara had a motive to kill Gulab. She was engaged to me but I broke off with her to marry Gulab. She took it hard, was a bit unhinged and was undergoing therapy with a psychiatrist. She could easily have killed Gulab in this mental state. Secondly, Sara's ear-ring was found next to Gulab's body. Thirdly, she got the drugged milk for me. Fourthly, the poison, which was used on Gulab, was found in her room. Fifthly, the police have even established that the poison vial was taken from her lab."

Sid paused for a second and then used a louder voice to add to the effect. "Now, let's say that a female with a figure like hers, wearing a dress like hers is seen on my balcony some time after the murder is committed, in the dead of the night. What will the police think? That she was there to get rid of some evidence! Even if it's not conclusively her, it does point towards her."

KD was about to say something when Tina broke in again.

"But…I still think… Upma…"

KD finally lost his patience. He threw a cushion at her violently before rising up and pouncing on her. He shook her hard and shouted at the top of his voice:

"Shut up! This is no time for your drunken talk! This is serious! What part of serious do you not understand?!"

He finally let go of a sobbing Tina to lie back on the pillows tiredly. He looked at her disgustedly while Sid tried to soothe her. Tina flung away from Sid and tears rolling down her face shouted angrily:

"You bloody swine! I am not drunk! I saw that bitch walking down the hall that night. I saw her with my own eyes! I saw her! I saw her!"

Both looked at her with horror-stricken faces and she added slowly and maliciously:

"And yes I was awake that whole night. Go tell *that* to the police!"

She grabbed the car keys and left father and son open-mouthed, looking after her lithe form.

A Dove with an Olive Branch

*A*cosy cottage on the hills in the middle of wilderness is the best way to describe Dulla House, Ned and Sara's farmhouse. Sitting in the veranda, sipping hot tea, one could endlessly gaze at the mountains that were so close. I felt I could just extend my arm and touch them.

I pushed at the door bell and waited for someone to open the door. After a wait of a few minutes and three more tries at the bell, I decided to try the door myself.

It gave way at my slightest push.

Once I entered the house the insides greeted me with an ambience both welcoming and simple. This room was playful, romantic and slightly elegant. A well remembered aroma whiffed in my direction, instantaneous and fleeting. It pulled me towards its origin and my feet followed where my nose led. I reached a colourful screen separating the living room from the rest of the house. The vanilla-musk here was so dense that it made me salivate. Someone was baking a cake.

"Uh….Hello!" said a soft cultured voice.

I jerked towards the voice and saw a petite girl with a tray of baked muffins in her hands, wearing a pale pink tunic with black slacks. She had a thoughtful, pensive expression lending her *a bearing of quiet confidence. But it was her eyes that gave her away. They were silvery grey with a slight hint of blue, just like her brother's.*

"Ah...I am sorry, I came in unannounced. I did ring the door bell, but no one answered," I said hesitatingly in order to explain my presence in her home.

"I'll get the cells changed," she said practically, brushing away my apology.

Ned and I had become good friends in the past few months. He had that rare combination of wit and intelligence with a depth of character belying his age. His ardent proposals of marriage were gaining momentum as each day passed.

And this time I had been unable to refuse.

I had been working in my office, deeply engrossed in understanding the intricacies of the current fiscal policies and their effects on my client when Ned called.

"Hi," I said in a singsong voice. He always managed to wake up the child in me. He was very perceptive and knew how I had always craved a father's affection; he treated me like a treasured little girl.

"Want to meet up, Princess?" he asked without any preamble.

"Are you in Mumbai?" I questioned.

"Could we meet if I am not?" He chided jokingly.

Now used to his teasing banter, I smiled into the phone.

"Our regular place at 6:00."

"What regular place?"

"Where we always meet," I explained patronizingly.

"I don't remember," he quibbled deliberately, tongue in cheek. We had met at least thirty times at a coffee shop in Worli, in the

last three months. It was near my office and on the way to my apartment.

"Of course you do," I said in a mock threatening tone.

"I just remember your little apartment," he said loftily referring to the day when he had cleaned up after I had puked on my carpet. He had never visited my apartment again, "I'll get wine. You are very fetching after drowning a bottle."

I could hear the smile in his voice and responded in an apparently snooty tone, "On second thoughts, lets drop the idea of meeting today; I do have some stuff needing urgent attention."

He laughed out loud, "Touché, ma'am, touché!"

He added, "Okay, don't draw your claws, Rose. Let's meet at the usual place."

"I don't have any claws," I acknowledged craftily, "Just a small dagger hidden in my purse." I couldn't suppress my laughter, "I'll have your blood."

"Then better become an enticing vampire and drink it. Don't waste it. Maybe like that Rosalie Hale from the Twilight series. I quite like her."

I laughed, "Sure."

Inwardly, I had always questioned Ned's motivation to want to marry me. I knew he was insecure about Sara's relationship with Sid. Marrying me was a sure way to keep me away from Sid forever. I knew how much he loved his sister. He could kill for Sara, so marrying me was not a big price to pay for her happiness. No one could fault me for being sceptical. So, I had carefully laid out my plan to never give in to his insistence. But as Mike Tyson has aptly said, everyone has a plan - until they get punched in the face.

I got punched in my face that same evening and all my plans went haywire.

Ned was dressed formally as ever though his short and spiky hair distracted from his serious image. His eyes lit up as he spotted me coming towards him.

He hugged me, droning softly in my ear, "Pierce slightly and drink away."

A waft of smoke lingering on his clothes filled my nostrils. But it wasn't repulsive to me anymore, it was kind of comforting.

"What?"

"Didn't we decide that you'll drink my blood and I'll pretend you are Rosalie Hale?" he pulled away laughing up his sleeve at me. I laughed my head off at hearing that.

I settled comfortably and ordered a hazelnut cappuccino.

"Still persisting on using a dagger, then?" he asked in all seriousness.

"I forgot it in the office," I made a sour face. "My bad!"

"There is another way you can have my blood."

"I am all ears," I played along.

He leaned on the table and surprised me by covering my hands with his bigger one.

"Don't husbands say that their wives drink their blood?" He added with a slight smile, "As an expression of harassment?"

He looked deep into my eyes and I couldn't control myself. I seemed to be losing the trail of time as I got a glimpse of his fathomless love for me. Today it wasn't hidden behind a curtain of control as it always was with only affection allowed to shine through the gauze. It staggered me somehow. I can't explain my reaction but I was convinced that I saw my fated stars in his eyes.

"Marry me, Rose," he whispered in a smoky voice.

He laid his free hand, palm up, on the table and added

*compellingly, "Hold my hand and from this day forward you shall
not walk alone."*

*The whisper created an intimacy between us and inadvertently
all the barriers of inhibitions broke for me. I knew I was going to
cave in but I tried giving excuses not only to him but to myself as
well.*

"But I don't want to go back to Ratnagiri," I said at once.

"You don't have to," he acceded.

"But you live there?" I persisted.

"I will relocate," he said without wasting a second.

"But you work there," I clutched at straws.

"I will work from here," he brushed away my objections.

*I sighed with a feeling of hopelessness. How could I ever forget
Sid? I voiced my thoughts with misery, "Ned, I don't love you. I
never can. That place in my heart is already filled."*

*His warm expression didn't freeze as I had expected. Instead, he
smiled softly and said:*

*"I don't need someone else's place, Rose. I am happy being where
I am with you."*

I chewed at my bottom lip with agitation.

*"We can have a great life together. I know it in my heart and
I think deep down you also believe it," he reasoned with candour.*

He beseeched, "Let us give it a shot, my Rose. Let us get engaged."

*As soon as he mentioned the engagement, a picture crept before
me unbidden; Sid offering a ring to Sara, bent on one knee and
declaring his love for her. I hastily pulled my hands away from his
grasp.*

"What about Sara?" I asked a tad too brusquely.

"She knows that you make me happy."

"*Are you willing to marry me for her sake? Because she is insecure about Sid's love?*" I voiced my greatest fear fearlessly.

"*You should know me better than that, Gulab,*" there was leashed anger in his voice.

The use of my given name instead of the one he preferred sounded odd on his lips. It made me feel rebuffed but I continued looking at him unflinchingly for a few minutes without uttering a single word.

His expression softened after some time and he said with emphasis:

"*I love you, Rose.*"

I thought about it for a while.

"*I would like to meet Sara before I agree to your request,*" I crossed my legs and sat back, "*Do you mind?*"

I wanted to find out for myself what Sara had to say about us. So, the very next day I headed to Ratnagiri and landed on her doorstep. And courtesy of the drained battery and her brother I entered her house and her life, respectively, unannounced.

Both of us kept on looking at each other uncertainly for a minute, at a loss for words. A beep from behind the screen drew our attention.

"*It's the next set of muffins. Come to the kitchen, if you like,*" Sara offered politely. I followed her to the other side of the screen.

"*I love this fragrance.*"

Sara turned towards me and smiled.

"*I know,*" she deposited the tray on a table and added, "*Ned told me that your apartment smells like vanilla.*"

I couldn't help but smile, "*My mother used to bake for me and our house smelled just like this. I don't bake but instead put a dash of vanilla essence on my lamp bulbs."*

Sara's mouth twitched at one side, which I later found out, was the characteristic way in which she expressed amusement.

"Ned said if I wanted to be friends with you I should bake you some mini muffins with vanilla flavour. They would surely win you over."

I was pleasantly surprised, "You baked for me?"

As an after thought, I added with yet more astonishment, "You want to be friends with me?"

She came close to me and clasped my hand.

"Come with me. Till these muffins cool down, let's talk and then I'll serve you some tea."

Still holding my hand she guided me out of a glass door. We crossed the back porch. It had rustic willow furniture and a painted swing. The cottage was littered with flowerpots, evergreens and other vegetation both inside and outside. We entered a glorious bedchamber, painted to resemble a gilded aviary. It was small and cosy just like the living room. We walked towards a piano and Sara offered me to sit on a recliner. She herself took a seat next to the piano and started playing a melodious tune.

"Like it?" Sara asked companionably after playing a few tunes.

"I loved it," I replied sincerely.

"Thanks. This piano is my mother's. She had real magic in her fingers." She smiled reflectively. "Ned and I were extremely attached to her."

"I was also very close to my mother," I touched the star shaped pendant around my neck lovingly. "This was her last gift to me. I have been wearing it for the last nineteen years. I never remove it."

"I know the feeling," she shook her head musingly. "Mom was our best friend. Now Ned and I try to fill Mom's shoes for each

other whenever needed." She touched my hand once again and said with utter sincerity, "Had Mom been alive, she would have welcomed Ned's love into our family whole heartedly."

She smiled lovingly. "Please marry my brother. He truly loves you," after a small pause she added, "and trust me when I say that I definitely won't mind. Sid and I will adjust to this new relationship with time. I am sure we can all be friends sometime in the future and forget the past."

And just like that, Sara, the white dove representing peace, offered an olive branch to me. She came on my arc, bearing hope for the beginning of a new life complete with love, happiness and warmth. And I accepted her offer with all my heart.

The Maid's Tale -1

"What were you doing in the corridor, outside the bedrooms, the night of the murder?"

Upma was a coarse, thickly-set woman with a shrill voice. She had come to the palace a few months ago after the old and trusted maid had gone to her village for a long overdue vacation. She helped keep the palace spick and span, slept in the pantry and assisted anyone who wanted a midnight snack.

After Tina dropped the bomb on KD and Sid that she had actually seen Upma in the corridor on the first floor that night, they had no choice but to interrogate the maid. Tina had taken off in her car, without her cell phone, and they couldn't reach her to glean any further details. The conviction with which she asserted her claims, however, left little doubt in their minds regarding her sincerity.

Upma answered in response to KD's gruffly asked question:

"Why would I go to the first floor at night, Saab?"

Her shrill voice grated on KD's nerves. He leaned back in his chair, stretched out his legs and used his most authoritative tone:

"Don't prevaricate, woman." He added severely, "You were seen in the corridor that night. We have a witness and if you don't want to be arrested by the police, answer me," he threatened. "Why did you go up there?"

Looking at her shifty eyes KD's suspicions intensified.

"Saab…I…I am not lying. I didn't get up at all that night." She fumbled with the *pallu* of her cotton sari.

Realizing the futility of this conversation, KD decided to use his pressure tactics. Without any warning, he stood up and prowled towards her menacingly, backing her into the wall. He growled in her face, his spit flying about with the force of his words:

"Don't you dare lie! You bloody moron!" He looked straight into her eyes, his eyes red with anger and without breaking eye contact shouted out to Sid, "Call the police, Sid! Lock this woman in the store."

As if enjoying the prospect, he said viciously:

"I'll see you hanged, old cow!"

The standing woman cowered under the attack and like a hen with ruffled wings, begged:

"No..No..Saab, don't call the police! Please! I'll tell the truth…..Please, Saab!"

Getting the reaction he had desired, KD settled comfortably in his chair once again.

Upma said very slowly in a shaky voice, "I took milk upstairs for Jack baba."

KD didn't know what he had expected but the simplicity of her answer didn't match his menacing expectations.

"Why didn't you say so earlier?" he asked authoritatively.

She thought for a few seconds, trying to still her quivering hands.

"Ah…..I…was afraid of the police."

The way she staggered through the sentence made KD's mind race.

"Who asked you to bring the milk up?"

She lied through her teeth:

"Ah…I thought the babies would need it."

KD picked up the phone on the side table and dialled a number. Conjuring up an indifferent attitude he simultaneously addressed Upma:

"The police will get the truth out of you now."

He spoke into the phone, "Inspector Sharma?"

Upma's eyes registered terror at the mention of police. She dropped down on her knees and appealed to Sid with fright.

"Chote Saab, I'll tell everything. Don't call police. Please!"

At Sid's touch on his shoulder, KD relented and put down the receiver. He said as an afterthought to Sid:

"Tell her to speak only the truth. Or else…"

With this threat hanging in the air, Upma's didn't deviate from the truth this time.

"Sara Memsaab came to the kitchen in the middle of the night. She needed milk for Jack baba. He had been crying. I got it ready in a few minutes and took it upstairs. When I reached her room, she was not there, and neither was Jack baba. Jill baby was sleeping. I kept the milk bottle on the side table and was about to go back to the kitchen when I saw Monica Memsaab coming down the corridor. She took the milk bottle with her. I went back to the kitchen and slept till 5:00 am."

"What was the time when Sara came to the kitchen?"

"I didn't notice it particularly but it would be just after 3:00 am."

Sid had an inkling now why she had kept mum but still asked to be sure.

"Why didn't you tell this to the police?"

"Ah….Saab….."

"Sara and Monica paid you to keep quiet. Didn't they?"

Upma spoke fretfully:

"I didn't mean any harm, Saab. Monica Memsaab said it would create unnecessary problems with the police. She couldn't have done the horrible deed and neither could Sara Memsaab, so I went along with it."

Sid was sceptical, "And money had nothing to do with it?"

She didn't answer and KD signalled her to leave. She turned towards the door, sighing with relief.

Sid asked of the retreating woman:

"Did you see or hear Jack crying?"

She turned back to him, "No, Saab. I thought by the time I came, he was pacified by his mother, to whom Sara Memsaab evidently took the crying child when she couldn't handle him anymore."

She left the room in a hurry.

"God be praised!" KD slapped his thigh with evident delight. "I can't believe we have *actually* found a witness to prove that Sara was awake around the time of the murder."

"What a respite!" Sid mirrored his jubilance. "This nightmare is finally going to end for us."

"I had been so worried. Speculation about the murder had caused quite a whirlwind on the professional front, with projects slipping from our hands, share prices declining and financial losses," he shook his head. "We seem to have avoided the potential threat to our name," he smiled happily.

"Narrowly, if I may add," Sid added brightly. The vibration of his cell phone drew his attention. "If it isn't Inspector Sharma!" he pronounced, looking at his father, "With more good news, I believe."

"Hello!" he spoke in a vibrant voice. But after listening to the other end his expression changed, lines of worry furrowing his brow. "But…that's not possible…I mean…Why would I steal the poison before the Charity Ball? I hadn't even patched up with Gulab back then. I know, I know…even Monica and Vikram had nothing to gain by stealing the poison…what? Only the three of us or the Dullas themselves could have taken the poison?…No one except Sara and Ned entered the lab after that?… and Sara's last record of working with cyanide was before the Charity Ball?…But that only means Sara herself took it…What does the police commissioner know? He is in Dulla's pocket…He thinks Sara would have replenished the poison had she taken it…Well, yes, if he has ordered you to investigate that angle, you have to…I understand…"

Listening to Sid, KD's fears returned with force. He could hear the tension in Sid's voice and his happy bubble busted. But what he couldn't hear was Sid berating his arrogant decision to walk up to Vikram and ask him to go to hell earlier in the day. On top of what Inspector Sharma had to say, if Vikram opened his mouth in front of the police, Sid's grave would definitely be dug; he shivered with dread.

Old Devil Moon

I

Sara came very close to becoming the sister I never had. I found out that beneath the façade of cool composure, Sara was a girl whose passions ran deep. She never gave away her true feelings, and even when seething inside with fury she could maintain a lady like decorum. Her life was composed of black and white. She either loved someone or hated him and that too with a fanatic passion, not in sync with the middle path or even understanding its import. This made her a fantabulous friend as well as a formidable enemy. We talked about everything under the sun except Sid. Neither of us broached his subject. This friendship made my life bloom. But just when I had thought that my life was coming together, I was awakened by a rude shock.

It all started with a Charity Ball.

It had been a week since my return to Mumbai. Ned had wanted to meet up but owing to some urgent work he couldn't visit me. Sara invited me for the Charity Ball in Ratnagiri and we planned to surprise Ned with my presence.

Chrysanthemum Hall was decked up for that night. This regal Ballroom was considered the quintessential venue for landmark events in Ratnagiri. Sara held onto my hand while walking

144

towards the hall, lending me support in her silent way. The lighting from the chandeliers enlivened the interiors with a dazzling array of magical colours. The effect delighted me as I caught a glimpse of our reflections in a wall mirror, quite surprised by the ethereal picture we presented.

Snow White and Red Rose walking together, hand in hand.

Sara was dressed in an ivory off shoulder gown in silk. For me, she had selected a bright red satin gown. With my hair hanging in tousled waves down my back and crimson lip colour, I looked vibrant.

I was appraising Sara when Monica rushed towards us, her friends in tow. Monica had never liked me and I was used to her acerbic comments. I didn't want to spoil my mood so I excused myself politely.

A light tap on my shoulder made me turn around.

"Yuvi," I hugged him tight, happy to see an old friend. The trauma of my past now forgotten along with my desire to never again talk to a Mehta.

"Happy, aren't you?" he looked closely into my shinning eyes, his hands on my shoulders.

I beamed at him. "Yes." Suddenly my eyes misted with emotion, "You know Yuvi, I have friends and a family, now!" There was awe in my voice.

"You always had friends." Yuvi's voice was clipped and his hands dropped to his sides.

"None except you." I touched his hand with affection. "I have so much to tell you. So much has happened in this past year," I excitedly pulled him to a corner, a child wanting to show off her lovely possessions. "I partied with Sara and her friends a couple of weeks ago. I was afraid that I would feel like an outsider in their

*midst, like I always did with Sid and his friends. But I didn't!" My
eyes lit up.*

*"You look beautiful, Gulab." Yuvi smiled softly. His eyes
traversed over my contended face. "Happiness is so becoming on
you."*

"Beautiful and me?!" I raised my eyebrows mockingly, "Liar."

"Look at yourself with my eyes," he smiled.

I waved off his complement and continued with my happy rant.

*"I am living a dream these days! A family!" My voice hardened
a bit, "I have felt like an orphan throughout my life. That conceited
family of mine always treated me like a cast out. They didn't have
anything else to give me except money…"*

*I glanced in my father's direction, seated a few feet away but
I didn't much care about him by now. I had found a new family,
which loved me irrespective of my accomplishments or lack thereof.
I turned away.*

*"We were your family, Gulab, weren't we?" Yuvi tenderly
touched my cheek.*

*I nodded with a sad smile, "Yes, the Mehtas were the closest
thing to a family in my life…"*

*Yuvi noticed my sadness and drew in an angry breath. "Until
Sid took everything away from you, that bastard!"*

*"Yuvi, it's alright," I tried to calm him down, "I have always
associated Sid with all the beautiful ties in my life. Didn't I meet
you through him?" I asked teasingly. "Had Sid not been there, my
childhood would have been unbearable and needless to say that I
am extremely grateful to him for those happy times."*

"You love Ned?" he asked directly in his no nonsense manner.

*I spoke after a minute, "We share this feeling of comradeship,
of caring." With a swift jerk I looked into Yuvi's eyes, asking for*

understanding, "Somehow, I know he will never let me down…"

I sighed loudly, "Sara and Ned have welcomed me into their circle of love and I feel whole again."

Yuvi kept looking at me silently, his eyes still questioning.

"I am extremely happy!"My lips curved in a smile of such brilliance that Yuvi couldn't help but mimic my expression.

"Always be happy, love." He hugged me lovingly and walked away, silent and strong.

II

I could see a lot of familiar faces as I looked around, huddled together in small groups with flutes of champagne gracing their hands, talking, laughing, dancing and generally having a merry time. My eyes were darting around for Ned. He made me feel like a woman and a child at the same time. He liked the weird rustic Gulab everyone else seemed to despise, much more than the chic sophisticate present in this party. I smiled shyly, imagining the pleasant surprise flitting on his face when he saw me, the excitement in his eyes when I would end his arduous wait and whisper my assent to be his wife.

I was in the middle of the crowded dance floor, when our eyes met across the room, Ned's eyes traversing over me, registering both surprise and pleasure at once and darkening with a little something more as he appraised my attire lovingly. My body instantly vibrated with something similar to an electric shock, tinting my skin with red, from the root of my hair to the tip of my toe. Shyness crept over me, unbidden, and I broke the eye contact at once, looking here and there for inspiration.

Around me the dancers started applauding as the fast number ended and a slow romantic track started playing in its stead. In an instant, someone tugged at my arm and Ned was blocked from my vision, my back towards him and I was enfolded into a circle of long sinewy arms. I could recognize that touch blindfolded and without even lifting my eyes to his face, I knew that I was in Sid's arms. For a minute, I forgot everything. I couldn't help just giving in to his embrace and follow his lead on the dance floor. He slowly glided me between the other dancers. I rested my head on his thudding heart and felt like I had finally come back home. He had been my home for eighteen long years; I couldn't stop myself from stopping in my former abode for just a few minutes. We just moved as one to the tune of an old classic, in the voice of Dianne Strong, from the 1947 musical 'Finian's Rainbow'.

His all too familiar, smoky voice reached me through the music, "The worst way to miss someone is when they are right beside you and yet you know you can never have them." He murmured in a thick voice laced with emotion. "I miss you, Gulab."

I did the unpardonable by letting my eyes shoot towards his beloved face and entangle in the chocolaty smoothness of his eyes. I wanted to but couldn't extricate myself from his magic and look away. The lyrics of the song playing around me sounded so apt and fitting.

> *"I look at you and suddenly, something in your eyes I see*
> *Soon begins bewitching me. It's that old devil moon*
> *That you stole from the skies. It's that old devil moon*
> *In your eyes."*

"Don't you miss me, Gulab?" He asked in a throaty whisper.

I wanted to shout that I didn't miss him, not at all, but a candid part of me reprimanded me and corrected that I did miss the person I had thought he was.

I didn't reply, just kept on looking into his eyes, drawn more and more into their depths each passing second, my happy childhood memories pushing me towards him.

> *"You and you glance*

> *Make this romance*
> *Too hot to handle.*
> *Stars in the night*
> *Blazing their light*
> *Can't hold a candle*
> *To your razzle-dazzle."*

"I haven't stopped loving you," his hand on my back pulled me tightly towards him. His cheek brushed my hair.

All the air left my lungs and my knees felt weak. Had he not been holding me, I would surely have fallen down. I whispered over his shoulder, more like a breathed sigh, "Sara?"

"Many are the stars I see, but in my eye no stars like thee," he whispered softly, his fingers splayed on my back, his warmth reaching me through the fabric of my gown. "I will have to marry her if you don't acquiesce to be my wife. I am sure you won't wish a loveless union on me."

He glided me expertly with the music towards the wall, away from the crowd.

> *"You've got me flyin' high and wide*
> *On a magic carpet ride*
> *Full of butterflies inside."*

"You and I are inevitable, Gulab. You're all that makes me happy. Come back to me, darling," Sid whispered appealingly in my ear, rubbing the nape of my neck tenderly.

As we were moving around the room, out of the blue, my eyes crashed into Sara's, over Sid's shoulder. Her eyes bulging wide, unable to believe what she was seeing, were filled with questions but her gaze was still hopeful and trusting of her friend. If she got to know what was in Sid's heart how easily she could turn inert and lifeless, I thought. Sid didn't love her. Their marriage would never give her any happiness. Sid had professed to love me. In that defining moment my life took a drastic turn. In that second I knew what I had to do.

Behind her was Ned, standing right where he had stopped in his tracks upon spotting me inside the ballroom. I sucked in a quick breath; his once warm loving eyes had turned into shards of ice, freezing everything that came their way. I turned my gaze away from him. I had to.

> *"Wanna cry, wanna croon*
> *Wanna laugh like a loon.*
> *It's that old devil moon*
> *In your eyes."*

I broke away from Sid.

"I'd be happy to come back to you, except it was you that went away," I answered with a smile. Behind that smile of mine, lay words left unsaid, words of longing, love, anger, hate and regret all repeating inside my head again and again.

> *"Just when I think, I'm free as a dove.*
> *Old devil moon, Deep in your eyes,*
> *Blinds me with love."*

CHAPTER – 24

The Last Word

I

KD and Sid were taking tea in the living room, sitting across the hall from Tina. She was in the dining room munching on a biscuit when she first caught KD's eye. She was being subjected to these sneak peeks from him when no one was watching for the last few days, she fumed inwardly. After a gap of a few minutes when she caught KD's eye on her again her temper soared. Initially she hadn't questioned him about this but now that they were not talking after the fight, Tina decided to tackle the matter.

"What are you looking at?" she shouted from her seat. "Is there something special stuck to my face that you are so interested in?"

Sid looked at her and then at his father unable to understand the outburst. KD got up from his chair and strode purposefully towards her.

"Don't you dare use that tone with me!" he hissed between clenched teeth.

"Then stop thinking nasty things," she replied heatedly.

"And how do you know what I am thinking?" he drew a chair next to hers and straddling it carelessly, met her eyes.

"It is evident in the manner in which you are looking upon me these days." She looked away.

"You mean looking upon you with suspicion?" he held her chin between his fingers and turned her face towards him daring her to meet his eyes.

When Tina didn't respond he spoke softly only for her ears, "My dear wife, don't think that I am not privy to your secret," he tilted her chin forcefully towards his face. "I know very well what you have got to hide and a selfish person like you can even kill someone in cold blood just to do that." He got up from the chair and added, "So, don't you pretend in front of me."

Tina bitterly addressed his back, "My arrogant husband, I won't pretend anymore but then neither will I let you."

He stopped and without turning asked calmly, "Is that a threat, *darling*?"

All he could hear was a bitter laugh and Tina sauntered out of the room leaving him to fume.

II

KD had been avoiding him since yesterday, Vikram's double chin bobbed with anger. He was about to join him when KD signalled Sid to follow him out with an imperceptible nod of the head, which didn't go unnoticed by the sharp-eyed Vikram. Had Sid ratted him out to KD after refusing him? He broke into a sweat. No, no, he couldn't, Vikram reasoned with himself, Sid certainly wasn't foolish enough to tell KD about his creditors just to spike Vikram.

Vikram had finally reached a momentous decision; to stop trying to find other partners. He was now left with no choice but to take his dream project forward with The Mehta Group. When he had been planning to somehow cut Gulab out of his business, he hadn't envisioned this predicament. His aim had been to find a way to let her go but hold on to her money by hook or by crook. He was even ready to share the profits with her. But not his throne. His lifelong aim of becoming the king was threatened by her presence. After living in the shadow of his father for years, slogging for a name of his own, he was still considered Watson to his father's Sherlock. And with Sid joining the family business his position had further deteriorated. He had everything except fame. And it was the one thing he could even kill for. The heart wants what it wants, he had reasoned with himself.

Now Gulab was out of his way and he realized her true worth. Her business acumen and foresight had been indispensable for this project alongside her loyalty. He had overplayed his cards in Gulab's case and this realization was eating him up. He had no one to blame except himself for this dire predicament; he clutched at his throbbing head. But he would not go down alone, he would drag Sid along with him, he swore vindictively.

"Helllooo! How's my new hairstyle? I just love these perms." Tina loved experimenting with her hair.

So lost in his thoughts was Vikram that his mother's presence on the sofa drew a surprised gasp from him.

She said jokingly:

"Lost in the thoughts of your beautiful wife?"

In his present state of mind he couldn't take her jest sportingly and retaliated:

"Learned it from you, my dear devoted mother. My father's slave!"

Not knowing about the altercation between them, he unsuspectingly touched a raw nerve. His mother said bitterly:

"Don't talk about that..that.. dirt bag! That pompous pig!"

Rarely did his mother use profanity, the sophisticate that she was. Vikram asked with concern:

"I don't mean to pry but did father and you have a fight?"

"Yes."

The monosyllable was all that she would yield. With a sigh she picked up the glass on the side table and tossed its contents back.

"That was scotch?"

She walked with her empty glass to an ivory inlaid cabinet and refilled it from a bottle placed there.

"You want some?" she asked offhandedly.

"No," he replied.

Her glass thudded on the wooden pub table as she carelessly lounged back on the sofa.

"You have been drinking a lot lately. Is there some problem?"

She laughed off his concern and tossed back another drink.

"Is there some tension between Dad and you?"

She looked at him with a steady gaze and a wicked gleam entered her eyes. She fingered the rim of her glass and with her eyes routed to her action, asked in a soft purr:

"Your Dad is hiding something from you, you know that?"

"He has been acting bizarrely. I noticed that…." He added contemplatively, "Maybe he *is* hiding something from me…. Humn…"

He asked eagerly, "Sid is in on it too, isn't he?"

Tina nodded and said with a sly smile. "You know why?"

He shook his head.

With a bite in her voice she replied cruelly, "Because you are your wife's faithful dog! You like whom she tells you to like. You do what she wants you to do. You fetch at her bidding. That's why!"

"You are drunk! Do you even realize what you are saying? Get up and I'll leave you to your room."

Though angry at her comments, he got up to help her but she laughed it off and nodded her head in a semi drunken stupor, "I don't think what your father thinks, baby. I know better. I saw you that night. I know what he doesn't...." she whispered in a secretive voice.

One more drink drowned in a gulp and she sighed contentedly. Closing her eyes she leaned back her head on the backrest of the sofa.

Baffled by her words but realizing that she was inebriated, he humoured her by asking:

"What do you know, Mom?"

"That no one else does."

She opened her eyes, put a finger on her lips and shushed him.

"Shushhhhh. It's between us. I didn't tell them anything..... nothing....I told them about that fat maid....but not you...... Shusshhhhh…"

The more she spoke the less sense it made to Vikram. He asked perplexed:

"What are you talking about, Mom?"

"Those fools think they are hiding it from you when you

have known it all along. You are hiding it from them, not they." She giggled like a schoolgirl with wicked glee.

Realizing his mother was too far gone to make sense, Vikram spoke to himself. "Hiding what? I am so confused."

Tina listened to his mutterings and replied in a daze.

"About me seeing that maid outside the bedrooms. What else, silly?"

After a pause she added, "I didn't tell them that you were also awake and went into Sara's room."

Looking at his puzzled face she bent closer to him and crooned in his ear, "On *the* night. After that frump you went into Sara's room. No doubt to implicate her."

She giggled again and slumped back on the pillows. "KD couldn't see what I saw…that you are no longer in your wife's clutches now…."

She laughed hysterically and chanted.

"You implicated her precious little sister….little sister… little sist…"

"Shut up, Mom! Shut up!"

Vikram got up angrily but before he could say any more, his mother passed out on the sofa. His black mood intensified as he understood the meaning of her ramblings. His only option now was to confront his father and find out the extent of the damage his mother had done.

He carried his mother up to her room.

"What the hell!" KD growled angrily at the sound of the door opening without a knock.

"As you can see my hands are full," Vikram raised his eyebrows defensively, "Mother has had too much to drink."

KD and Sid had been immersed in a deep discussion and

KD's disposition worsened at seeing Tina in his room. Sid came to where Tina was lying serenely on the bed and looked over her anxiously. "Mom has been drinking way too much since the murder. Haven't you noticed, Dad?"

"Your mother has been drinking excessively for the past couple of years but I believe you guys have been too busy to care."

He looked at Vikram shuffling from one foot to the other.

"What is with you? Nervous about something?" KD asked casually.

Vikram had been thinking about how to broach the subject with his father and Sid. He had to find out what his mother had been feeding them. Stiffening his resolve he delved forth with an offensive strategy.

He took a seat next to Sid, folded his one leg over the other and with a pretentious calmness, which he was far from feeling, said in an injured voice, "You didn't need to hide it from me. I can keep secrets. Even from my wife."

Both KD and Sid's eyes opened wide but they didn't react in any other manner.

"What are you talking about?" Sid asked in mock puzzlement. His resentment at being blackmailed had washed off after having a conversation with the Inspector. He wanted to get back in Vikram's good books but without giving him too much information.

"You don't need to carry on with this façade, Sid. Mom was drunk and she blurted it all out."

Sid was still looking at him with the same quizzical expression. With a half smile, Vikram pronounced each word slowly, "About....the.... maid!"

"Trust that loud mouth to spill the beans!" KD looked at the prostrate form of his wife and his voice filled with contempt.

"I hope you are not like your mother," KD's words hurt Vikram. Vikram's gut wrenched at the thought of KD taking over his project and for the millionth time he cursed himself for being too greedy.

Instead of showing his hurt and anger to them, he shrugged smugly, "That's for you to find out, Dad."After a pause he added, "I thought you were a good judge of character." He arched his eyebrows, "Should I reconsider?"

KD's eyes twinkled at that but he kept his mouth shut. Sid moved closer to his brother on the sofa and faced him squarely. He was a sales wizard and reading people correctly to find their weakest spot was easy enough for him. He assumed a softly reassuring voice and consoled:

"Pillow talk can be very dangerous for us all at this point. Your wife's loyalties lie with her sister and she is doing everything she can to save her." He continued emotionally, "Gulab was so young, just twenty-four......She could have been blissfully happy today, had she been alive. But that chance was snatched away from her. Because of a jealous woman! I want Sara to be hanged!"

Vikram touched Sid's shoulder and looked directly into his eyes, "Sid, you should know, I stand with you on this and not with Monica. If Sara killed Gulab, she will be behind bars. How can you think I want something other than that?"

He added with emotion, managing to conceal his self loathing, "She was my business partner and my friend too. With her gone I have lost my dream forever. I can never forgive whoever killed her."

The truth of his words sank in as soon as he uttered them.

Yes, he could never forgive Gulab's murderer. Never, he sighed tiredly.

KD said:

"We just didn't want to risk our family's safety by taking a chance. Monica can easily exploit this situation to Sara's benefit and your mother's detriment. We can't let the police try to pin the crime on Tina. I am sure they won't be able to prove anything but your Mom is not emotionally stable right now. We need to protect her."

"What exactly did Mom tell you?" Sid asked.

For the next few minutes they exchanged notes.

"Why was Mom awake the whole night and how did she manage to see the maid without getting noticed herself?" Vikram was perplexed.

Sid shrugged. "She won't say. I have asked her umpteenth times."

Vikram got up from his seat and rushed out into the corridor. "I'll just check out the corridor." After a few minutes he returned huffing.

"The plan of this floor is in the shape of an irregular octagon. The landing of the stairs forms the first side of the octagon, leading to Dad and Mom's room on the left, their bedroom being the second face of the octagon. The main bedroom leads to a boudoir via a connecting door here."

He indicated the door leading to the smaller room.

"The boudoir opens onto the balcony, facing the front gardens. This balcony can also be entered through the reflecting glass doors opening from inside the corridor. These glass doors are the third face of the octagon."

"We know that as well," KD exhaled loudly, "You needn't

tell us."

"I am thinking aloud. Just listen."

Vikram continued musing.

"Just next to these glass doors is Yuvi's room sharing a common wall with Sid's room. Both rooms have their separate balconies looking over the pavilion and lake. Both these rooms form the fourth face of the octagon. Just parallel to these rooms on the other side of the corridor are two guest rooms. These rooms don't have balconies. Ned was staying in the room opposite Yuvi's. This room is just next to the landing of the staircase, on the right side. Sara was in the room opposite Sid's. Both these rooms form the fifth face of the octagon."

Sid again tried to interrupt him but Vikram put up a hand to signal him not to disturb his flow of thoughts.

"Right next to Sara's room is a staircase going to the second floor. The door to this floor is always locked. This is the sixth side of the octagon. Next to this staircase is my room, a mirror image of Dad's room. Instead of the boudoir we have a children's room opening to a balcony facing the parking lot. The glass doors from inside to this balcony form the eighth face of the octagon."

KD said impatiently:

"We know the layout of the bedrooms."

"I was just reconstructing the whole thing in my mind," Vikram nodded to himself in a pondering manner.

"Why?" KD asked condescendingly.

"To locate Mom's position. Why is it that she could see the maid but the maid couldn't see her?"

Sid's eyes lit up. "Yes, it can give us an idea as to what Mom was doing that night."

All three of them went into the corridor and scrutinized the whole area for some time.

KD opened the glass doors of the balcony of his room and went outside. The balcony had a small wicker table and a few cane chairs littered around. KD was walking towards the banister when his foot struck something. Near the leg of a chair a glass bottle had been resting before KD toppled it with his foot. It was empty. He picked it up and took it to Sid.

"Sid, look at this. It is your brand. Is this from your bar?"

He offered the empty cognac bottle to Sid. Vikram also joined them.

"Yes, it is from my side bar, out of the new stock. I stocked it up before the wedding. But I haven't kept it here or drowned its contents."

"I can venture a guess at who did," KD said scornfully.

Sid nodded, "I think Mom has been drinking it."An idea popped into his head, "Do you think Mom was sitting here that night? Look, no one can see her if she sits near the wall."

He moved a chair in the position and dropped down on it.

"Vikram, check from outside if you can see me."

Vikram roamed the whole corridor and came back to the balcony.

"No, you are not visible from outside."

KD pronounced:

"Then this is where your Mom was sitting that night."

Sid asked bewildered.

"But why couldn't she just say so at the outset? At least to us, if not the police!"

Vikram didn't meet their eyes. "God only knows!"

KD said, "Let's go back to my room."

Once in the comfort of his air conditioned room, KD's face took on a judicial, appraising look.

"So, Tina did see the maid that night, confirming that Sara and Monica were awake at the time of the murder. This doesn't prove anything conclusive against Sara and definitely nothing against the maid. She just brought a bottle of milk for Jack, kept it in the room and left."

A sleepy voice drawled:

"But she didn't have the milk bottle in her hands when she was coming up the stairs."

Their eyes jerked towards the bed. Tina's eyes were half closed and she added with a simper:

"That fat cow was looking left and right standing on the landing of the stairs, like crossing a road."

She giggled:

"Except she looked like a fugitive. A cow fugitive! Ha! Ha!..... And then she tripped over her *sari* and fell down...."

She laughed with mirth and her eyes closed a fraction more.

"No bottle in her hand.... The cow used both hands to get up. I saw. No bottle. The cow should go to a gym...."

KD threw up his hands and sighed with frustration.

"She was drunk that night, just like she is now. We can't trust her on this."

"Male chauvinistic pig! I am the witness here and the last word this time is *mine,* not yours. Mine. Mine....."

Her eyes closed fully and in a few seconds she started snoring loudly, leaving them to infer the meaning of her revelation.

Overdosed on Guilt

I'*m a firm believer that sometimes it is right to do the wrong thing and I hesitated for just a heartbeat before doing just that at the Charity Ball. My decision overdosed my heart with guilt that whole summer. The remorse of hurting my friends was not letting me sleep in peace. Oblivious to my predicament, Sid was keen on celebrating our impending union. He had declared his desire to marry me at the Charity Ball itself and I had accepted his request. Sid wanted me to start a life with him on the Royal Hill and wrapping up my life in Mumbai didn't take long.*

I was going to the palace, the first time after we had reconciled and my heart started pulsating wildly at the thought of facing the Mehtas. There was a time when it was the most natural thing for me to visit them but now I felt like a stranger, an imposter, trying to wheedle my way into a close knit family. I alighted from the car and saw Yuvi, sitting on his haunches and polishing his bike. He ran towards me with childish delight, throwing away the brush in his hand and greeting me with open arms.

"I missed you," he hugged me tight.

Sid was guiding me towards the stairs and Yuvi made a sour face at him, "Why are you rushing away with her? Give us a few minutes to catch up."

"Dad and Biji are waiting," he replied shortly and Yuvi threw up his hands in a yielding stance.

"Whisk her away then," he looked at me with a soft smile, "but we'll have a long heart to heart before you leave." I nodded my assent and Yuvi went back reluctantly to his bike.

As I was climbing the stairs, a though struck me and I turned, about to shout something out to Yuvi. He was standing by his bike, the windshield bag embossed with a set of Harley Eagle Wings opened, and holding tenderly a small yellow and white stripped glove with the image of a Mickey Mouse etched on the palm. He was holding it like a newborn, tenderly and with love in his eyes. My earlier thoughts forgotten, I hurried down the stairs dislodging Sid's hand on my back.

"Hey! That's mine," I snatched the glove from him. "You are up to your old tricks, stealing and hiding my stuff. When did you steal this?" I asked with mock anger.

Sid was quick on my heels, "What happened?" he asked ruffled.

"This is my glove," I waved the small woollen thing at Sid. "I lost it one fine day, years ago and couldn't find it," looking at Yuvi in mock anger I added, "Your brother stole it, I found out today."

"I found it lying around the gardens and guarded it for you, dear," Yuvi snatched it from me and zipped it safely back in his windshield bag, adding flippantly, "I just forgot to return it. After all these years protecting it, I have earned the right to keep it."

My mouth agape at his temerity, I retraced my steps and added over my shoulder, "I am happy that you can't wear it, at least."

He laughed up at me and I giggled in response while following Sid inside, my nerves forgotten in this jovial banter. The family was seated in the lounge area, waiting for us and a combination of glaciered smiles and warm hugs greeting me into their midst. I had expected as much. KD Uncle and Tina Aunty were all smiles, congratulating us. Vikram welcomed me like a long lost family member, engulfing me in his bear like embrace. Her glasses dangling from the gold chain, Biji sketchily wished us luck but her eyes clearly stated otherwise. Monica sneered at me from afar not deeming it worthy to talk to the husband stealer she thought I was and sat silently in a corner after partaking from a glass of champagne as KD toasted to our love and impending marriage.

I was standing alone in a corner, my thoughts occupied by my conscience speaking up, when Vikram brought me a bowl of ice cream. I politely declined the proffered treat. He took me aside and spooning the chocolaty concoction hurriedly in his mouth, spoke in an awkward manner, ill at ease with the situation.

"What I was asking was," he spooned another mouthful hungrily, "ah…I want to start a new project…ah…not a family project," he looked guiltily towards his father and finding him deep in conversation with Biji he continued, "This is confidential. Between you and me. You understand?"

I nodded politely.

"Ah…I can't ask Dad for help," closing his eyes a little, he spoke hurriedly as if trying to get something off his chest as soon as possible, "Can you help me? Financially, I mean?"

Opening his eyes, he added hurriedly, "We will be partners, of course. And I promise you that we will draw profits out of this project."

How I thanked God for that opportunity! I always had a lingering suspicion that I won't be able to pay off my debt to Vikram but destiny presented me with an opportunity to do just that. I was overjoyed.

"We can sit and discuss the project details. You can check the feasibility yourself," Vikram spoke quickly, taking my silence as a sign of denial.

I hastily spoke to set his mind at rest, "How much do you need?"

He named an astronomical amount. I instantly calculated that I would have to sell most of my assets to get that amount. My mother's alimony and the money fixed for me had been well invested over the years. Combined with that the real estate prices had risen tremendously and were still on a high. I decided instantaneously to sell it all off even if it meant a few personal losses for me.

He added, "Not all at once. For the first phase we would just need half of this money."

"Ok, partner." I offered my hand smilingly.

For a minute Vikram was taken aback. He asked staggered, "You don't want to check out the details of the project before agreeing to this?"

"You want to undertake this project?" I asked.

"Yes."

"Then we will take it up."

He took my hand in a hearty shake, excitement brimming from his every pore. He had made me experience the love of a protective sibling that Christmas Eve and it was my turn now. I did everything possible to help him get his coveted project. We needed political clout as well as money. For the first time in my life I asked my father for help. His influence was enough to help us cut through the competition.

Once we had acquired Vikram's dream project, the only thing left for me to do was to make it a success. KD Uncle was right; Vikram didn't have the capacity to do that alone. He had needed my help desperately even if he did everything possible to negate the fact. I wasn't interested in taking control of his empire. I had already decided to help him build a strong foundation and then melt away from the picture. Vikram couldn't decode my intentions correctly and by tricking me he tricked his own destiny.

The Maid's Tale - 2

KD and Vikram were sitting in the boudoir waiting for Sid who had gone to fetch Upma. With a burning desire to save him family name, KD was at sea about how to sort out the whole mess. Sid's desire to extricate himself from getting convicted for his wife's murder knew no bounds. And Vikram's only wish was to snare Sid back into his web somehow and finally build up his own kingdom. But time was not on their side; all three of them had only four days left to amass their desires and trick their impending ruin.

Fiddling with his i-phone, KD declared:

"I know how to go about it."

After a few seconds he kept his phone down and turned to Vikram.

"Grab the key to the store room."

The store room was a dark and damp room on the second floor which was rarely opened a few times a year, filled with old junk. A few minutes later he returned with the keys.

The door to the boudoir opened and Sid followed Upma into the room.

Without any preamble, KD got up and said:

"Follow me. And don't speak on the way. I don't want to

invite attention." Once reaching the second floor, KD shut the door to the stairs behind him, cutting them from the rest of the household. Upma noticed it and her breathing became heavy. Sid fiddled with the electric switches and a solitary bulb threw its weak light on the whole floor. They seemed to be moving towards darkness now and Upma's steps began faltering.

"Saab, where are we going?" she asked haltingly.

None of them answered her. Sid propelled her forward by her arm, half dragging her with him.

"Please Saab! I am afraid of the dark…" she tried to dislodge Sid's hand without any success.

Paying no heed to her KD undid the lock of the store room. All of them entered and KD switched on the single tube light fixed on the wall. He closed the door after them and indicated Sid with a flick of his hand to move away from Upma. Looking directly into her bulging eyes, he picked up a metal rod lying on the floor and walked ferociously towards her, his eyes on fire and the rod raised in an attacking stance. Upma took a few paces back, shaking with terror.

"No Saab!" She closed her eyes tight and flinched with fright, her hands rising protectively over her face.

With a loud grunt KD brought the rod down. The air ruffled by the force of his action and stirred Upma's body but the rod didn't hit her. Instead it smashed the tube light on the wall, and its glass scattered on the floor filling the room once again with a sinister darkness.

Upma opened her eyes and her racing heart settled into a smoother pace until she heard KD's terse command.

"Now she will stay in the dark she is so afraid of, until the police reach the palace to arrest her," he sneered. "Lock her in."

Barking this order at his sons and with a final snarl towards the alarmed woman, he rushed out followed by Sid and Vikram. Upma ran after them managing to reach the door as it slammed harshly on her face.

Alone in the ominous darkness, sniffing the damped muskiness of the ever closed room and feeling the presence of slithering lizards and cockroaches crawling towards her, Upma was scared stiff. She was paralyzed with fright as something crawled near her feet, not daring to move for fear of touching the slithery reptile. The dreaded being climbed over her prostrate body and she shrieked wildly, closing her eyes tight with dread. The fear of this horrid atmosphere mingled with the threat of being arrested finally registered with her and as her terror took concrete shape in her imagination she started banging on the door, crying to be let out.

"Please Saab! Please….let me out!"

No one responded to her entreaties. She crouched on the floor with her ear pressed to the door to listen for anyone on the other side who would succumb to her pleas. Upon hearing the sound of footsteps outside, she renewed the pounding with vigor.

Her cries for help converted into sobs after a few minutes. She fell to the floor and shouted heart wrenchingly:

"I know ….I …I ….lied. But I didn't kill anyone…."

Upon hearing her buckle under pressure, KD smiled crookedly. He decided that it was time to increase the pressure and break the woman completely with a final blow. He pressed a button on his i-phone and the siren of the police jeep started tearing the place down.

The dread in Upma's voice was now evident as she cried:

"No! No police! Please! Stop them!"

After a few more sobs she continued:

"I'll return the ring, Saab. You have a big heart, Saab, please forgive me....don't send me to the police. I'll give it back. I haven't sold it. Please! I became greedy but I will never do it again. Oh!!!"

Her voice cracked and her howls engulfed her speech.

The three Mehta men looked at one another uncomprehendingly. Finally KD asked noncommittally:

"When did you steal it?"

She replied within sobs:

"That...night...when I brought the milk bottle to Sara Memsaab's room. I had seen her beautiful jewels kept on the side table. As I went down I was thinking if I could also have some beautiful things like rich people when this evil entered my head," she hiccupped. "No one was in the room and so ...so...ah...many jewels were kept there.....all lovely...Oh so lovely....I thought, if only I could own one such beautiful thing...if only....," he gulped. "The devil clutched me then and I thought if I would pick a small item, no one would notice or care. After all, rich people have so many things. Why couldn't I take just...a... a small trinket from them. And considering the hustle bustle of marriage functions no one could pin it down to me," she sighed. "So, I turned back and took the sm..smallest thing. A silver ring."

She took a gulp of air and her voice filled with awe as she remembered the stunning bright and colourful jewels she had touched. She added whimsically, "There was this beautiful gold necklace with red stones...," he eyes brightened and the dread of the dark room receded, "and the matching big earrings, gold bangles embedded with multi coloured stones, bracelets, anklets and other small things," she smiled reminiscently. "I loved the set Sara Memsaab was wearing for the wedding.... but I didn't take it, Saab," she added pleadingly. "It was too costly. I am not a thief, Saab. I just took the silver ring. The cheapest thing. Not to sell but just as an object of beauty.... I couldn't resist, Saab...I couldn't..." She broke into tears once again.

KD ordered:

"Let her out."

A shaky weeping Upma came out and fell down on KD's feet.

"I know I did wrong, Saab, I'll return the ring. But please don't hand me over to the police. Please, Saab," she pleaded repeatedly.

"Stop this drama," KD commanded harshly, "You will work only in the gardens from today. Don't dare enter the palace or try to leave the Royal Hill. And as soon as this investigation ends, you will leave the palace and never show us your face again."

He turned to Vikram.

"Tell the gatekeeper to keep an eye on her and take the ring from her possession."

Vikram went down with Upma and KD and Sid returned to the boudoir.

"You think she is telling the truth?" Sid asked his father.

KD nodded.

"Upma was acting in a shady manner because she stole a ring and not because she is an accomplice to the murderer. Monica had been asking everyone about Sara's ring but I never really considered the fact that someone could have stolen it. I thought she had misplaced it and would find it sooner or later."

"Mother was right though. That woman is a stupid cow. She took away Sara's solitaire thinking it to be a silver trinket! And the other jewels Sara wore for the wedding were all artificial. The earrings and necklace wasn't rubies set it gold. It was just imitation…to match her dress…..."

Sid broke in mid sentence and his forehead furrowed in thought. He rushed out of the room. Reaching the landing he caught hold of Vikram and Upma.

"I'll accompany her."

Vikram shrugged offhandedly. "Okay."

As soon as they reached the servant's quarters, Sid closed the door after them and pounced on Upma with his query.

"The jewels Sara wore for my wedding were there on the table when you picked up the ring?"

She replied in a small voice.

"Yes."

"You remember her gold and red jewellery set?"

When she nodded her head in affirmative, Sid demanded:

"Describe it to me."

"Why, Saab? I swear I didn't take that! I swear!" she insisted beseechingly.

"Just describe them," Sid ordered much like his father would have.

Upma started in a feeble voice but as her thoughts drifted to those ornaments, her voice filled with awe and she described the beautiful articles every woman wanted to possess in great detail.

"The necklace…'

He cut her mid sentence.

"The earrings, describe them."

"They were beautiful. Big dangling ones. With egg shaped red stones in centre and small pearls around them. They were set in gold."

"Both the earrings were there?"

"Yes, Saab."

There was dread in her voice as she said:

"I swear, Saab, both of them were there when I left. I didn't steal them. I just tried them on and the necklace too. But I kept them back on the table. I swear! I just took away the ring. You can check my trunk if you don't trust me!"

"Are you sure you tried both earrings on?"

"Yes, Saab. I tried them both on. I looked so good wearing the whole set. I saw myself in the mirror and then removed them all and placed them back on the table. I didn't take them. I didn't!"

Sid opened the door and stepped out, a bit dazed. He muttered distractedly:

"It wasn't Sara. Sara isn't the murderess."

"I could add that much up," a voice pronounced triumphantly. Sid's eyes widened in shock upon finding Vikram standing in front of him. "I followed you, obviously."

He continued, "On a serious note, let us reassess the situation. The official time of death is between 2:00 am and 4:00 am. And the major evidence against Sara was that earring. Upma saw them in Sara's room around 3:30 am. It proves that Sara had already removed her ear-rings at that time. If Gulab was killed after 3:30 am, why would Sara put them back on just to kill Gulab? And if Gulab was already dead before 3:30 am, it is clear that Sara has been falsely implicated, as she has been professing all along, by deliberately dropping her earring near the body. One of her earring was obviously stolen from her room after the maid left, to implicate her."

"Why didn't Mom see the person who entered Sara's room after Upma left?"

"Firstly, she was drunk. And secondly, she didn't know she had to be on a vigil. She just happened to see Upma purely by chance. And then she may have drifted back to the bedroom."

"The maid's story exonerates Sara of the crime. Someone obviously planted her earring and the same can be said about the poison found in her room. And the same person could have stolen the bottle of poison from her lab also." Sid threw up his hands in defeat. In an aggrieved voice, he asked, "But then who killed Gulab?"

"I don't know that," Vikram shrugged. "But what I do know is that if you don't want the police to replace Sara's place in their report with your name, you'll reconsider your decision to help me out." Vikram smiled derisively, "The game is back on. Three days to go!"

Was I Forgiven?

*T*he announcement of our marriage, two months away, coincided with the season's first rain. I could hear the thunder roll in the distance. Showers of gentle rain pelted on the rooftop, tapping softly against the aged window panes of my father's house. I inhaled the fragrance of the freshly drenched earth deeply, rejoicing in its earthy perfume.

My feet, with a mind of their own, involuntarily led me out of the house and towards the road, tracing the path of the rivulets I had been admiring from my room. The gray skies mirrored my mood. Walking aimlessly, lost in thought, I saw something which instantly shook me out of my trance. I realized that I had walked to the outskirts of the town near the Dullas' farmhouse. I had walked at least ten kilometres in the pouring rain. The rain had now stopped but I was soaked to the skin.

Looking from my vantage point from the end of the path leading to the Dulla residence from the local market, I saw coming towards me the two well remembered and loved faces; Ned and Sara, huddled under colourful umbrellas.

I had my choice; I could have turned and run off or faced them both heads on. I chose the latter alternative and took the ascending path leading me towards my friends. It had started drizzling once again and I tilted my neck, catching the rain drops on my face.

It was then that I saw Ned's eyes fall over me. I surprised in the depths of his eyes the same emotions I had witnessed that day at the Ball when he had first caught sight of me. It felt as if he had forgiven me. In those few moments I felt somehow at peace with myself. The last thing I remember before losing consciousness and hugging the cloudy darkness was an ardent desire for rain every single day of my life.

I woke up in the middle of the night, in a fit of feverish haze, babbling something unintelligible. I repeated again and again in disjointed sentences, "Ned, Sara...forgive me....please..." Strong hands pressed me back to the bed, crooning softly in my ear and calming me. A feather light caress on my cheek made me snatch the warm fingers touching me and I buried them under my cheek comfortingly and went into the embrace of sleep once again.

A bright ray of sunshine and happily chirping birds greeted me to a fresh new dawn. I rubbed my heavy eyes and found myself in a room painted to resemble a gilded aviary. It was Ned's farmhouse. I looked around me with confusion; I was still trying to make sense of my situation when the bang of a door drew my attention. I pushed off the quilt and found my body snuggled in a warm green tracksuit. It was big enough to be Ned's and smelled reassuringly of musky smoke. My shoes were nowhere to be seen so I padded towards the noise, barefoot. I followed the terrain leading to Sara's laboratory.

The door to the lab was half open and I walked in unabashed but a reference to my name made me freeze in my tracks. An open wooden cupboard hid me from the view. The pungent smells emanating from the bottles filled in the cupboard, neatly labelled, made me want to sneeze badly and I automatically covered my nose with my hand.

Sara's voice was edged with pain as she spoke appealingly to her brother, "I know you are distressed, dear. But you can't blame her for everything. Both of us knew in our hearts that Sid never got over her."

Ned, unable to meet her eyes, shouted back, "She was your friend" he shook his head with frustration. "She owed you her loyalty."

"I have been in her shoes," Sara smiled disparagingly and added, "You remember how easily she forgave me?"

"She wasn't like a sister to you back then. You didn't owe her anything," he clenched his hands with anger, "I can't forgive her!" Ned blurted.

"Ned, she has always loved Sid. Both of us should be happy for them," Sara stressed, turning her back to her brother so that he couldn't witness the pain in her eyes.

"Your therapist has fed you this crap?!" Ned thumped the shelf angrily with his fist.

"Ned…" Sara started in a placating voice but Ned cut her midsentence, realizing how insensitive he had been, talking about Sara's psychiatric treatment. She was still going for the therapy sessions recommended after her nervous breakdown. Outwardly she seemed much better but Sid knew how raw her wounds still were. He turned towards her and hugged her unawares.

Over her shoulder he whimpered, "How can I forgive her for those miserable weeks you spent huddled in your room, crying for days on end? How can I forgive her for what she made you suffer? The humiliation! The heartache!"

Sara cringed at the remembered grief, but composing herself, she replied:

"I have forgiven her, Ned," she lied. "And so can you. I don't want you to feel this excruciating pain because of me. You can be

friends with her if you want," with determination she added, "In fact I would like that very much; to be friends with her and even Sid and the Mehtas. They are our relatives, after all."

His arms tightened around her.

"Sara, baby, you are the most important person in my life. I can never befriend the person who has hurt even a hair on your head, let alone someone who has shredded your dreams," his eyes were hopelessly antithetical to his words, filled with the pain of longing. But he was a strong man and he crushed the small voice prodding him to accept Sara's offer.

"That is why you couldn't sleep the whole night, your eyes staring unblinkingly at her face, your hand cupping her cheek for hours?" Sara moved away from him and asked sceptically, with a twinge of anger in her voice.

"You don't mind what she did to you, Ned," she spat, "if you can forgive her for breaking your heart, why can't you forgive her for breaking mine?"

"She hadn't accepted my proposal and I had given her a choice at the onset of our friendship. She was free to marry anyone she loved. She was never mine," he stressed, "but she owed you her loyalty. No, I can't forgive her. Ever."

Sara knew that she had to make Ned forgive Gulab. She just had to for her plan to work.

Her voice was lined with urgency now, "Ned, if you love me, forgive Gulab. I know you want to."

"Fuck her!" he spat. Ned never abused and the extent of his hurt was apparent to Sara.

Burrowing behind the cupboard, I heard it all and even I could absorb the pain I had made these beautiful people go through. I had a strange involuntary reaction to Ned's ire. The stress of the *last few months took to me at last. I wanted to end it all. End my life. The hate emanating from him was proportional to my desire to get away from it. I couldn't bear to witness it in his eyes. My eyes darted desperately around the room. I wanted to find an exit, a way out. In the flurry of commotion that ensued, a vial dislodged from a neighbouring shelf, breaking into small pointy pieces. In my haste, I trampled over it barefoot, running out of the lab, my hand in my pocket and shards of glass embedded in my feet, blood spurting from them.*

Sara and Ned looked after me in horror, my feet marking the floor red, shouting for me to stop. Ned took after me and caught my staggering form in no time. He carried me to a chair, depositing me carefully in it, like an infant. Sara got a first aid kit and fussed with my wounded feet for the next few minutes, Ned standing over us. Strangely enough, her ministration didn't hurt me in the least, my attention focused on the strong hand clutching my shoulder, sighing loudly with pain every time Sara plucked out a shard of glass from my skin. Hope surged in my heart and life seemed bearable once again.

It seemed at the time that I was eventually forgiven. Was it just wishful thinking on my part?

Lost or Found?

'Desperate times call for desperate measures.' Repeating it again and again in his mind, Sid pushed the door bell. A servant boy who knew Sid well opened the door.

"Saab is not at home but Sara Ma'am is in her lab. Should I call her for you?"

Sid nodded and the boy left him alone in the living room. He took a seat near the window and gazed unseeingly outside.

"What are you doing here?" Sid jumped at hearing Sara's voice after a few minutes.

He stood up and walked a few paces closer to her, "I came here to apologize."

She scoffed at his reply and her elfin body shook with anger. "I don't care," she spat at him, albeit ladylike. "Get lost!"

Sid took a few more steps near her. With only a chair standing between the two of them, Sid could look closely into her eyes. They were swollen and red with dark circles under them. Regret climbed on his back, weighing him down with its onus. He tried once again with a smile:

"Won't you ask what am I sorry for?" Without giving her time to reply, he continued hurriedly, "You could never have killed Gulab. I know that now and I am very sorry not to have trusted you before," he apologized humbly.

The sincerity in his words and the earnestness in his eyes touched Sara. The burden of being incriminated for a crime, the suspicious glares of people wherever she went, the muttered words behind her back and the insinuations of being a murderess had driven her to a state of extreme sensitivity. The relief which came with someone believing in her innocence broke the barricade of her pent up emotions. She fell back on the sofa, her hands covering her face and sobbed her heart out.

Sid tried to reassure her but his commiserations fell on deaf ears. He waited for her to cry out her troubles. Finally she controlled herself and after taking a few gulps of air, looking away from him, asked politely, "What made you change your mind?"

"The truth."

Her eyebrows arched with curiosity.

"I found out about the bribe you and Monica offered to keep that maid quiet," he stared her down. "And you should be thankful for that."

"Ah!..." She looked away guiltily and added after a few moments, "We just didn't want to be embroiled with the police. We didn't….didn't kill….."

Taking pity on her, he said simply, "I know you didn't kill Gulab."

He dived into his pocket and held out Sara's ring.

"This is yours, I believe."

Sara accepted the proffered item and nodded her head awkwardly, remembering the discussion with her siblings. The thief was the murderer. She didn't know how much Sid knew and without giving anything away, she asked casually:

"I misplaced it that night. Where did you find it?"

Sid looked at her closely. "I don't think you misplaced it, as you very well know. It was stolen from you just like your ear-ring."

He told her everything he knew and concluded it with his assertion, "If you had come clean in the beginning, all this won't have happened."

"We were scared that the police would connect us with the murder if they knew we were awake that night." She said after a pause, "The maid could have easily stolen my ear-ring along with this ring. She was the one who discovered the body in the morning. Maybe she murdered Gulab and implicated me." She finished animatedly, gaining confidence with every word she spoke.

"It is a possibility. But Yuvi was just coming down the stairs when she came back in, after finding Gulab. She was so distraught that she fainted before Yuvi's eyes. We discussed it with him and he says that either Upma is a brilliant actress or her distress was very real. I tend to believe the latter. Plus she had no motive to kill Gulab," he finished in a contemplative voice.

"There may be a motive which we do not know of yet. She is definitely a suspect for me." Sara was adamant. "I think she had already done the sorry deed before I went to the kitchen…"

Sid cut her midsentence.

"Sara, Yuvi says Upma didn't notice him on the stairs. She came running into the living room using the back door and with a small shout fell on the floor. If there was no audience, why would she be acting?"

Sara was obstinate, "What does Yuvi know? He was irked by tiredness and sleep deprivation. That cunning woman definitely fooled him. She knew he was on the stairs."

"You are clutching at straws and you know that," Sid said with force.

"I know no such thing! Yuvi's AC was not working that day. The poor guy was opening all the windows to his balcony when I went down to the kitchen to get the ceremonial milk. His door was open and he was swearing at the electricians who fixed those decorative lightings. Ned was already fast asleep; otherwise both of them could have shared Ned's room. I offered to wake him up but Yuvi refused. I bet the mosquitoes didn't let him sleep well. To top it all, he had been in an accident as well. So, you see, Yuvi could easily have been mistaken. He was not his usual alert self that day."

"I know about the air conditioner. You have managed to confuse me…"

"The magician, who can puzzle both the innocent maidens and sophisticated damsels alike with tricks of mind and hearts, is confused! Kneel to this magnanimous day!"

Her joke was tinged with hurt which she tried to cover by sarcasm. Had she said this a month ago, Sid wouldn't have been able to cut to the pain behind her statement. He would have taken it as a mordant comment, at its face value. But today her anguish reached him and being the perpetrator of her pain, he couldn't stop being remorseful.

"Sara," he said with feeling, "I…I have been a jerk. Selfishly taking what I wanted without a care about right or wrong. With you I behaved abominably," he shook his head with self disgust and exhaled furiously. "I can't help but think that this is my punishment." He looked into her eyes and with a great effort said very slowly, "I have to make a confession." He sighed, "Contrary to what everyone thinks, I didn't marry Gulab because I loved her."

"But...," Sara stumbled over her words, so shocked was she by this revelation. "You told me that you wanted to break our engagement because you loved her."

He just shook his head in negation as if to say that he had lied.

"I thought that Gulab's love had changed you," her voice was edged with aggravation. "That is why I found it so easy to forgive you. I thought you had changed for the better and I was happy for Gulab...."

She wanted to strike Sid with her bare fists. Sara loved her brother Ned to distraction. He had sacrificed his love at Sara's insistence that Sid loved Gulab. Sid had spoiled both Ned and Gulab's life. She couldn't help but think that Gulab would have been alive today had she not married Sid.

Her voice scorched with anger at this callous man sitting opposite her, "Why then? Didn't you know that Ned loved her with all his might? She would have been happy with him," Sara's fingers curled tightly in a small fist.

Sid replied simply:

"I thought what I felt for her was love. I sincerely thought it was love," he was earnest in his insistence. The vision of Gulab at the Charity Ball flashed before his eyes, her flawless skin had accentuated her big hazel eyes, long curly locks of dark hair hung loose down her back, grazing her tailbone and something about her full luscious lips had just fazed him. He had to have that delectable damsel in red.

"The imbecile that I was, what did I know about love? I couldn't even begin to fathom the depth of its fervour. If I had any idea about its truth I would have steered clear of it," he laughed without any mirth. "But then how could I have experienced the most beautiful and enigmatic thing a man can feel? You know, these days the first thought in my head in the morning when I wake up is she; my last thought before I go to bed is also about her. It is like I have stopped existing and she lives somewhere inside my heart, a part of me," he jerked back to look at Sara and said with a sad smile, "Love came unbidden to me. When I least expected it. It found me the day I lost Gulab."

He sighed sadly. "Don't sages and saints say that we reap what we sow? I played with and broke a lot of hearts and this is my punishment. The agony of not having the one person you want above all else; the anguish of separation from your love. No one can imagine the extent of my pain, my sorrow. I can never be whole again. This is my sentence, isn't it?"

Sara could just stare at him after this profound revelation. All her earlier misgivings vanished into thin air. Her eyes filled with pain for him.

Again Sid laughed mirthlessly, "The magician you professed me to be a few minutes ago, is again confused." He asked sadly, "Did I find love that day or lose it? What should be the right expression, Sara?"

Sara patted his hand consolingly. After a few minutes of companionable silence, she spoke gently:

"Whatever has happened cannot be changed. All we can do is to punish whoever took Gulab away from us."

Sid nodded his head. Out of the blue he blurted, "I know about the red hair on my bed that Monica found," Sara looked at him astonished. He continued contemplatively, "I thought it was yours at first. Now that I know better, I can't seem to establish whose it could be."

"Only Ned and I have red hair…."

Never Marry but for Love

*T*he *Mehtas had plans of throwing an elaborate wedding bash for Sid and me but I clearly put forth my views on the subject to Sid. In respect of Maa's memory, I wanted an extremely simple marriage ceremony as per Sikh customs at the Gurudwara she used to frequent as a child in Paonta Sahib, her paternal home. Though disappointed, he gave in to my demands and I graciously agreed to a grand pre-wedding function and an even grander reception ceremony.*

The festivities started with Shagun, engagement ceremony, which marked the beginning of the wedding celebrations. The Ratnagiri Palace sparkled for the occasion with the shimmer of satin, the bright colourful flowers, the strands of lights, the subtle aromas of scented candles, the laughter of the elegantly attired guests and the chords of chic music.

Getting ready upstairs I could hear the party in full swing. Sitting amidst an array of professional makeup artists and hairstylists my eyes were seeking desperately for a friendly face. In the midst of this flurry I was feeling extremely lonely, deserted somehow.

"Close your eyes," the makeup artist commanded, while one of her assistant offered a pallet of eye shadows to her. Confident strokes of cool brush stained my eyes within minutes and I opened them to a sigh of approval from her.

Blinking my eyes I gazed in the mirror and caught sight of Yuvi, peeping discreetly from the door. Ignoring the people around me I ran to fall into his open arms, hugging him tight. He signalled the party of helpers to leave us alone.

Drawing in a deep breath as if finding courage to voice his opinion, he said:

"Sid doesn't deserve you, love."

"Sid will change one day," I added in a confidant voice.

His voice hardened a notch, "He is unabashedly flirting with Sara downstairs." He added angrily, "And that girl has some nerve showing up at your engagement party!"

"Sara and Ned are here?" I lit up with pleasure.

After ministering to my wounds, Ned had silently driven me home that day. I couldn't gather enough courage, after hearing his scathing comments, to ask for his forgiveness though every time our eyes met he glimpsed the regret in them. My downcast eyes and a pensive expression had conveyed what my lips couldn't.

Yuvi shook his head. "What are you so happy about?" he asked with incredulity. "Don't forget that scheming bitch took Sid away from you and she is trying her best to snare him away now!"

"Yuvi!" I admonished, "Sara is a friend."

"How could you be friends with her?" Yuvi clutched his head with frustration, "That bitch is trying her best to seduce your fiancé!"

"We are good friends," I maintained adamantly.

Yuvi screeched, "Can't you hear what I am saying? She is flirting unabashedly with Sid downstairs. At your engagement party!" he grasped my hand. "Just looking at the crass dress she is wearing makes me want to cringe." Yuvi persisted albeit softly, "She is bent on seeking revenge from you, love. That is why she is here."

"I also took away her fiancé, Yuvi." I smiled sadly.

"That is different!" Yuvi responded vehemently.

I laughed softly upon hearing his reply and hugged him once again with affection.

"Don't worry, Yuvi. Sara doesn't mean any harm." I rubbed his back comfortingly, *"And thanks for taking care of me, my friend."*

A discreet knock on the door and the entry of the event planner signalled the end of this conversation. He advised me to get ready in the next half hour. With Yuvi standing beside me, like a doting mother, the next few minutes were full of teasing banter and laughter for me.

Once ready, Yuvi escorted me downstairs. As I was walking down the stairs my eyes darted around the room trying to catch a glimpse of Ned and Sara. After a minute of careful scrutiny, my gaze fell on Sid, his back towards me. A girl with a smooth creamy back, dressed in a very short backless black dress was hanging onto his arm. Out of the corner of her eye she saw me coming down the stairs, our eyes met and reality dawned on me. She was Sara, though not the tasteful and refined Sara I knew her to be. Clutching Sid's hand, she deliberately tugged him towards the library door. Yuvi saw me looking at the retreating couple and clasped my hand in silent support. A sneak peak at him made me realize the intent of his resentment at their behaviour. His eyes shot murder, blood red, and nose flared with anger.

"I'll kill Sara if she hurts you again, Gulab. I promise I'll kill her!" He swore thickly, in a slow seething voice meant only for my ears.

As soon as we descended the stairs, a bevy of well wishers crowded around us. A few minutes later Sid came pushing through them to reach me, Sara by his side and a smeared stain of lipstick *mark near his lips, smothered but still visible. The colour matched Sara's lips, crimson. I deliberately moved to the side of the stairs, muttering an excuse to the small crowd around us, with Sid, Sara and Yuvi following me.*

Within no time Ned disentangled himself from the midst of a small group and came towards his sister. His eyes at once grasped the situation, Sara's hand resting lightly on Sid's arm, her lipstick mark on his face and a wild triumphant look in her eyes.

Sara came towards me, a conniving smile on her lips and naked hatred in her eyes and offering Sid's hand to me said in a deliberately sweet voice, "All yours."

Her smirk said it all. Sid was an unfaithful bastard.

Yuvi muttered something in Sid's ear and both of them left through the back door.

Ned instantly grasped Sara's arm, shocked at her behaviour. He had earlier been surprised at Sara's choice of clothes but given her state of mind he had just taken it as an effort to show off her indifference to the world. But looking at her performance just now, he knew better.

He reprimanded in a slow censorious voice, dragging her away with him.

"Sara! Come with me."

"Hey!" I addressed Ned in a mock scolding tone, "Where are you taking my friend?"

I clasped Sara's free hand tenderly and looking directly into her eyes spoke earnestly, "I wish I'd been a better friend to you."

Sara just kept staring at me for a minute, the humility in my eyes finally touching her. Her tough sneering expression began to fade, very slowly, with every word I spoke.

"Words will not be able to ever express how sorry I am," I sighed

sadly. "Will you understand if I say I couldn't stop myself, though I wanted to? Love does this to you, doesn't it?" I asked painfully. I repeated once again, with a touch of self-condemnation, "I'm sorry for everything I put you through."

Sara didn't utter a single word and shaking off my hand moved towards her brother, "Let's go, Ned."

Both of them left the palace that day but they didn't leave my life. A day before the wedding, Sara came to my father's house with a brightly wrapped gift in her hand. I was sitting with a mehendi artist, decorating my hands and feet in traditional Indian patterns.

"Sara!" I had gotten up excitedly to greet her, my hands still moist with henna.

She hugged me tightly, minding my hands and kissing my cheek.

"I couldn't stay away, Gulab," her eyes filled with tears, "I am sorry for the…" Her voice broke down, cheeks red with shame.

"Hey!" I soothed her softly. "You don't need to apologize, dear. I understand. Only too well," I spoke in a choked voice.

Controlling my emotions, I added jokingly, "You know, you can kill me and I'll still say that you don't need to apologize."

Sara had bought with her traditional Punjabi bangles, chuda, *for me. We chatted like old times for an hour before she left me with a promise to attend my wedding and bringing Ned along with her. Shamefacedly, she also revealed that she had tricked Sid into accepting a peck from her on the cheek and he had behaved like a perfect gentleman with her.*

It seemed like she had forgiven me. Eventually.

The Lost Star

Unknown to both Sid and Sara, Ned stood near the door listening in on their conversation. He had wanted to hurl Sid out of his house as soon as he saw him sharing a sofa with his sister. Nose flaring with anger he charged towards Sid but stilled in his tracks as he heard his ardent admission of love for his dead wife.

Ned looked hard at his sister, checking for any sign of romantic feelings for that unfortunate bastard sitting next to her. All he could see was sympathy oozing out for an old friend. He didn't want this empathy to transform into a more potent emotion. He vowed to speed up the process of moving back to London which he had already decided upon after discussing with his sisters. He knew his yearning for Gulab would accompany him wherever he went but at least Sara would get a chance to forget the rough patch of life she had witnessed in the past year, he thought.

Ned's ears pricked with Sid's last comment about the red hair and his senses instantly stood on alert. He couldn't let the conversation drift towards the presence of that hair. He deliberately shuffled his feet noisily. Sara's head instantly turned towards the noise and upon finding Ned standing there, she signalled him to join them with a small gesture of her hand.

"What is he doing here?" Ned asked Sara instead of throwing a direct question at Sid, blatantly displaying his bitterness for him.

Sid replied before Sara could, "I came to tell you that Sara's name is cleared in Gulab's murder case."

This managed to clear the air immediately between both men. When KD had appointed Sid as the head of sales in his company, the astute man knew what he was doing. Sid had the knack of tearing down people's defences by any trick of the trade. He was a creative and effortless deceiver. Sid knew that direct neat approach would work with the sensible and practical Ned just like he had known that Sara couldn't resist the sentimental exchange that had just taken place between them. Once Ned's defences were down, it was not difficult for Sid to make him open up and talk. They probed into evidences and discussed a few scenarios.

Befuddled, Ned closed his eyes tight and rubbed his throbbing forehead. "Someone is pounding my head with a thick hammer!" he complained, still massaging his forehead.

"You haven't been sleeping at all, Ned. Please take an aspirin and rest for some time," Sara was all concern for his brother.

He lit a cigarette and puffed on it for a minute before replying, "My vivid dreams won't let me sleep."

"What dreams?" Sid asked interested.

Ned looked at Sara over Sid's head and her eyes remonstrated with him for the slip of his tongue. Neither of them wanted to tell Sid that Ned's dreams were filled with images of his dead wife.

Sara quipped with a giggle before Ned could reply, "Ned is having nightmares. We used to dream about ghosts when we were children and sometimes when Ned is upset he still has the same nightmares. Isn't it funny?"

Sid nodded and his eyes widened in comprehension of what had been happening to the twins at home.

"Oh! So it is a twin thing! It all makes sense now. Jack and Jill are having some nightmares too. At first I was highly sceptical. How can two different people have same dreams? But if you two had them too, then I think it's a possibility with twins," he misinterpreted Sara's words. "They have made it into a game. We were thinking about consulting a psychiatrist, but now I am not too worried," he smiled briefly.

Sara had made up the story about the nightmares to cover up for Ned. Now the twins looked at one another, confused.

Sara asked, "What nightmares are they having?"

Sid replied with a little surprise, "I thought you knew all about them. They started the night…," he gulped, "….Gulab died. Jack was crying that night because of this nightmare."

"And Jill had the same nightmare?" asked Ned.

"Yes. Though their dreams are not exactly same. It would have been really spooky otherwise."

He continued with a laugh, "Both of them hide under cloaks and tie scarves on their hands and try to scare us all by clawing like a ghost. The funny part is that they say they have seen ghosts and they dress like this. They even had a fight one day over the colour of the ghost's scarves. Jack said it can be any colour and Jill thinks it is the colour of Biji's bandages."

As if remembering an important fact, Sid said excitedly, "One of them thinks that even you have been dreaming of the same ghosts. I don't seem to remember who proclaimed it."

Sara smiled. "What tales these little devils cook up!"

Ned said with a smile of his own. "They remind me so much of us when we were kids."

"We had so much fun at the expense of our nanny. She used to call us 'crazy brats'," both of them laughed out loud, immersed in remembering their childish pranks.

"You remember that piano teacher of yours, the fat one with huge glasses? How I used to twirl her thin ponytail and put chips in her handbag while she tried to instruct you."

Sara admonished, "Don't make me remember. I got all the scolding from her because I couldn't stop laughing and you never got caught. I can't play the piano extremely well like Mom and I completely blame you for it. You never let me learn."

Sara stopped in mid sentence. A vague memory hit her out of the blue, a memory of Gulab listening to her playing the piano, Gulab talking about her mother. What else had she shared with Sara? What important fact had just knocked on the door of her memory but was now evading her? She forced herself to remember that day again.

"What happened, Sara?"

She put a finger on her lips, indicating Ned to keep quiet. She remembered that day again. How beautiful Gulab had looked sitting near the piano, talking about her late mother and showing Sara her pendant.

Yes! It came back to Sara. What had Gulab said? That she never removed her pendant. It was her mother's last memory. If she never removed her pendant as she had professed so many times, why wasn't it found on her body?

She asked Sid breathlessly, "Where is Gulab's pendant?"

Both Sid and Ned looked at her uncomprehendingly for a few seconds before her meaning sunk in. Both of them had been close to Gulab and knew her fetish about her mother's last gift to her.

"It wasn't found on her body," Ned said thoughtfully. "It may be in her belongings, but I strongly believe that she was wearing it that night, like always."

Sid said:

"She was definitely wearing it for the wedding. She never removed it in the last nineteen years, why now?"

"Unless she didn't remove it," said Sara thoughtfully, "but someone else did."

"Who?" asked Sid.

Sara's voice had a sinister intonation and she pronounced with conviction. "Her murderer."

Sid went home after an hour long discussion and a promise to search the palace for that pendant. Ned stood a minute or two looking after him. He shook his head slowly and thoughtfully.

"I think Sid is play-acting. I have a strong suspicion that he killed Gulab," Ned pronounced.

"He was drugged," Sara pointed out caustically.

"Was he? We have only his word that he drank the milk. He could easily have mixed the pills in the milk himself and then spilled it down the drain."

Humpty Dumpty had a Great Fall

*M*y *mother used a very simple trick to make me have my food when I was a child. She used to say, "Eat your vegetables or the crow will fly away with them. He loves to have your food." Hearing this I would gobble up the dish that I abhorred otherwise.*

Maa understood human nature. There are certain things which we consider our own and although we don't appreciate them, we still don't want others to enjoy them. They are ours. *As soon as we see someone else craving for them they start tempting us as well. But when the other person's interest dwindles over time so does ours.*

I too was such a morsel of food for Sid. To think that he married me because he truly loved me would be just too optimistic. Sid's interest in me was kindled when he saw the plain girl of Ratnagiri transformed into a classy young lady of Mumbai who was desirable and drew appreciative glances from all. To add fat to the fire a sought-after bachelor had proposed to me. He knew only one way to reclaim what he thought was rightfully his. To marry me.

A treasured relationship is like a delicate ornament. If you have it, it gives you the same pleasure that an exquisite piece of art gives you, drawing the attention and envy of all others. If you don't have it you feel incomplete, knowing that you lack an object of beauty. But the most precarious situation is when after getting it, we adorn it as a centre piece and someone carelessly topples it over, forgetting its fragility.

Usually when a relationship breaks because of deceit, lies or selfishness, bitterness creeps up unnoticed and takes refuge in the once pure heart. It induces misery and tears. But when the shadow of this adulteration darkens by repeated strokes of perfidy, the grief switches into anger. Sad people just cry over their condition but when their anger flares, it shakes them up and a desire takes root in the depths of their hearts. A desire to inflict what they have suffered.

So, yes, relationships are like glass, complacent when cherished and irreplaceable once trampled on. It is advisable to let the broken glass be than hurt yourself trying to put it back together. And even if you want to, could humpty dumpty ever be put together again?

It was the day of my wedding when one such humpty dumpty had its great fall.

A Silent Call

I

A warm blanket wrapped tightly around him, Ned was sitting on a wicker chair on his front porch, overlooking the mountains in the distance. The sun had already faded and the little embers of light coming from inside the house were the only illumination in Ned's dark and dreary world other than the silvery gleam of the moon playing hide and seek with the dark clouds.

Sid had rummaged around the palace for Gulab's Star, searching vigorously in all the rooms, both public and private, but to no avail. The pendant was nowhere to be found. It was as if it had traversed the other world along with its loving owner. There were lots of loose ends to be tied, Ned sighed tiredly. A cool, crisp breeze ran through his hair and he pulled his blanket higher around him. He tucked his feet underneath him and snuggled deeper into the cushy chair, slowly closing his eyes and allowing himself to rest in the tranquillity.

He opened his eyes to a mesmerizing clang of glass bangles somewhere near him. In the dim light he saw a figure standing a few feet away, gazing at the stars, and her profile towards him. The cool gentle breeze ruffled her hair, blowing them over her face and making it almost impossible for Ned to peer closely at her. As if understanding his predicament, turning fully towards him she brushed the unruly strands away from her face. The light of the moon fell on her for a few seconds before she turned away once more, intent on gazing at the starlit sky. It didn't take more than a split second for Ned to recognize Rose. He immediately got up and ran towards her, dropping the blanket behind him. 'Catch me if you can' she seemed to dare him, retreating into the bevy of trees and merging somewhere with the horizon.

For minutes Ned was unsure of what had really happened. He questioned himself repeatedly. Had he been daydreaming or had it really happened? Was his desire for Rose so great that let alone his dreams even his waking hours were now filled with her memory? Being in the present state of emotional turmoil, he was not really sure of the facts anymore. All he knew was that he had a burning desire to find her.

He ran inside for his car keys and hastily pulling on a leather jacket left the farmhouse. He drove recklessly on the moonlit rambling roads of Ratnagiri, his scrunched eyes looking around for Rose at every bent of the curving road. He drove like a maniac before finally reaching the gates of the Ratnagiri Palace.

He was about to drive away when he thought that he heard a whisper at the window of the car; someone calling out his name. But there was nothing but darkness outside. He heard the voice once again, from afar this time, the other side of the gate. Without much ado, his brain frozen into submitting to the mesmerizing voice, he entered the palace. The gatekeeper opened the gate for the familiar face without any protest.

His ears attuned to that slow melodious voice, Ned drove

very slowly through the winding driveway, all windows pushed down, so that he could stop his car as soon as he heard the whisper once again. He reached the covered porch in no time, still trying to pursue the call. Now extremely restless, thinking he had somehow lost track of Rose, he jumped out of the car to look around for her in the gardens. Like a madman he ran around the front gardens, stopping at every creak of a reptile or rustle of the leaves, listening intently for more to follow. The moon was now completely eclipsed by the clouds and a chill had started to seep into his canvas shoes from the wet dewy grass. Deflated and tired he stepped on the paved driveway and automatically started following its contoured form.

The clouds drifted over the moon, a portion of it now visible and throwing light on the lake. Ned's feet automatically led him to the placid water body. He looked at his reflection in the depths of the murky water in the pale moonlight. A man with hollow eyes and a grim expression stared back at him. He seemed like an alien to Ned, nothing like the cheerful contented man he used to be. He thrashed at his reflection with a branch cutting through the water with anger. The unsatisfactory image was washed away with the ripples giving way to an undulating image in white. It was hazy, unclear and rose and fell with the small waves created in the water. But it was easily recognized by Ned. He looked away from her reflection in the water to where she should be actually standing, somewhere over the bridge. To his disappointment there was no one there. He looked back at the water and even her reflection was gone replaced by the same hollow-eyed man. Ned was berating himself for his overactive imagination when he heard the clang of glass bangles once again.

In the silvery moonlight he saw her on the Pavilion. Dressed in one of her Punjabi suits, curly locks falling over her back, she was trying to attract his attention by clinking together her bangles, a sound which Ned had always adored. Ned stared at her, perplexed, not sure what to do. He rubbed his eyes to check if his imagination was once again playing games with him.

The apparition laughed, throwing back her head. It floated on the wind towards him, the sound of church bells, pristine and light. He was sure now that it was his Rose. Afraid that she'd do her disappearing act once again, he walked very slowly over the bridge towards her, as if trying not to scare her away, and stood a few feet away from her.

"Why did you go away, Rose?" he asked slowly in a pain smeared voice.

She smiled like an angel and moved behind him. He could smell her perfume from there and breathed in big gulps of it, closing his eyes and revelling in her proximity. When silence greeted him for a few more seconds, he turned to face Rose and found to his utter despair that she was gone, nowhere to be seen. He looked around him desperately. His eyes searched the Pavilion, the bridge, the gardens and finally moved towards the Palace. Standing in the middle of the Pavilion, he could see only two balconies from there. The curtains from one of the room were flowing outside the windows, rustling in the wind. Behind them Ned thought he saw his Rose standing. Leaving no time to deliberate over the matter, he took to his feet, running towards the back doors and rushing up the stairs.

The room was not locked and in his haste, Ned walked in without knocking. The bed was occupied but there was no one on the window. He rushed towards the balcony and stepped outside. There was no one there. His gaze drifted towards the

Pavilion and he thought that he saw his Rose waving to him from there. At a second glance, he could see no one there, just a silent dark night and an empty Pavilion. But for that split second he had thought that she was saying her final goodbyes before leaving him alone forever and his heart sank as soon as that thought struck him. He couldn't afford to lose Rose, he breathed sadly.

Ned sank down on the floor of the balcony thinking about her; their first meeting, the night in her apartment, the Charity Ball and finally her wedding. He was recreating everything that had happened that day before his eyes and smiling sadly, remembered her. It was then that the pieces began fitting together; the pieces of the puzzle.

The facts started making sense to him; the Pavilion being visible from only two rooms, Sid's drugged milk, the stolen poison from Sara's lab, the lady on the balcony and that red hair on Sid's bed.

His head throbbed with so many ideas that he didn't know what was right and what wasn't. But one thing was certain in his mind now, he had not been hallucinating when he saw Rose. She had come to guide him. And she had guided him to this balcony.

Till dawn broke on him, he sat there on the floor thinking things through. He tried to remember everything carefully. The more he thought about it, the more his convictions solidified. Ned now had an idea about what had happened that day, his instincts guided him. But there were still some gaps which needed to be filled, some facts that he had to verify and some proofs that were to be collected. Ned waited desperately for the sun to rise.

II

"Where were you?"

Sara rushed out to confront Ned upon hearing his car enter the driveway. Stress and worry creased her otherwise smooth forehead.

Ned alighted hurriedly from the car and clutching her hand preceded her into the living room.

"I was worried sick," she berated him. "Where were you the entire night?" Sara repeated.

"At the palace."

"But…" Ned cut the litany of questions about to sprawl from her with a swift shake of his head and a muttered entreaty.

"There is something extremely important that I want to discuss with you," there was urgency in his voice as he sat down next to her on the sofa. "Think carefully and then answer my questions."

Sara nodded her head mutely.

"When did you last see that vial of potassium cyanide in your laboratory?"

Her forehead furrowed, "I distinctly remember taking out that vial a day before the Charity Ball. I never touched it after that day."

"Did you lock the cupboard afterwards?"

"I never lock any cupboard in my lab. The main door is always locked when I am not inside. As you know I never ever leave the lab open when I am not around, not even for coming up to the house for a few minutes."

"Humn…"

Ned pondered on her reply before speaking thoughtfully.

"So the person who stole the vial must have done it

practically in front of you."

"I think so…" Sara said uncertainly. "But only Monica, Vikram and Sid visited me in the lab on the day of the Charity Ball. After that day no one except you and me entered the lab."

Ned nodded.

"There is another question, think very carefully and then reply," Ned cautioned. "While you were preparing the ceremonial milk in the kitchen, did you leave it unattended at any time?"

"No," Sara was positive. "I did go to Biji's room to get some saffron to put in the milk which she had procured specifically from Kashmir, but that was before I started preparing the milk. Before retiring to bed, Aunt Tina specifically asked me to undertake this task. I was surprised to say the least, considering that I was a guest. A maid could easily have taken care of it. "

"Was there someone around you in the kitchen?"

"Not a soul."

Ned got up instantly. Moving towards his room, he spoke hurriedly:

"I have to talk to the children and then get ready and reach the palace as soon as possible. Inspector Sharma is going to submit the report tomorrow," he said over his shoulder. "I will tell you everything in the evening. Bear with me till then."

III

Both Jack and Jill were ready for school and having cereal in the dining room at the Palace.

"Hi kids!" Ned replied with a smile, offering a huge bar of chocolate to each of them.

"Can you help your Uncle Ned?" he asked cajolingly.

"Sure thing," Jill replied, spooning cereal into her mouth.

"You remember the day your Aunt Gulab got married?" He continued after the children nodded: "Who amongst you cried in the night that day?"

"Jack. He is a baby!" Jill replied tongue in cheek.

"She also cried the next morning. She is also a baby," Jack was quick to retaliate.

"Why did you cry Jack?"

"I saw a ghost," he sucked at his lips.

"Ghost!" Ned feigned fright. "How brave you children are!" he looked at them with awe and the twins beamed back at him happily.

"I have never seen one. Will you tell me how ghosts look like?" he asked in a pleading voice.

"Okay!" Jill nodded happily.

"Was the ghost male or female?"

"Male," Jill pronounced.

"He wore glasses?" Ned asked.

Jack laughed at him. "Ghosts don't wear glasses! You know nothing, Uncle Ned. Ghosts are tall and strong like He-Man."

"What about his face? Was it gruesome?" Ned asked, trembling with terror.

"He didn't show his face. His face and shoulders were cloaked with a shawl," Jill licked milk off her spoon.

"He covered his whole face?"

"Silly!" Jill simpered, "The ghost mostly had his face away from us. Away from the bed."

"Facing the bureau-table?" Ned slipped in adroitly.

"Yes," Jack bit into a tomato sandwich.

"What was the ghost doing in your room?"

"Um…He was moving in the room. He had scary hands… with masks…."

Ned took out a crepe bandage from his pocket and showed it to them.

"Was the mask like this?" he asked.

"Um…" Jack looked towards his sister. "Maybe. Jill says it was."

"Both of you saw him?"

"Yes!" They nodded importantly.

"I am scared of this ghost!"

He kissed them goodbye and then walked purposely towards the library. He opened a cabinet where he knew all the photo albums were generally kept. The wedding album was placed atop the mound and crouching on the floor, he flipped through it carefully. His eyes lit up as he found what he had expected all along. He slipped out a picture from its transparent holder and dropped it into his pocket.

His work at the palace done, Ned was about to enter his car and drive away when he heard Yuvi's bike roaring in the distance. Yuvi came to a halt near Ned's car and nodded curtly in his direction.

"Hello. Yuvraj, driving at the pace as you do, without a helmet at that, can be quite dangerous," Ned cautioned in a friendly tone.

"How does it matter to you?" Yuvi responded offhandedly. In the past Yuvraj had liked him but Ned could feel that after Gulab's death, their equation had somehow changed. He had attributed it to the allegations against Sara but now that her name was cleared, Ned hadn't expected this rude behaviour.

"I just meant that you do quite a few stunts with your bike and an accident without a helmet can be life threatening," Ned replied in the same friendly manner pretending not to care about his rudeness.

"Life," he sneered, "Don't care about this barren, so-called life." As if realizing that he had spoken too much, Yuvi tossed evenly over his shoulder, "Don't worry I won't die in an accident. Haven't had one in the last six months."

He walked briskly towards the front door, leaving Ned looking after him thoughtfully. He waited for Yuvi to walk inside the palace before commencing with his actions. His work done in a few minutes, Ned entered his car hastily and went back to the farmhouse. For Ned the rising sun had brought with it a probable solution to the mystery surrounding Gulab's death, a hypothesis, which Ned knew in his heart to be the truth. It was the truth told to him by Gulab. Who would believe him if he told them about his meeting with Gulab? He hadn't believed it himself the morning after. Anyway, he had resolved to prove what he already knew had happened.

He had to show everyone the truth.

He owed it to his Rose.

IV

"I don't believe all this!" cried Inspector Sharma. He stood up from behind his desk and started pacing his office. At last he dropped back in his chair and faced Ned Dulla with some consternation.

"What you are saying is preposterous, Mr. Dulla," said Inspector Sharma. "How can you expect me to believe such a far-fetched tale?"

"I have proofs right here with me, Inspector," supplied Ned. "Why don't you just look at them and then decide for yourself?"

For the next few minutes, Ned calmly explained everything to the police officer once again but this time intermittently pushing towards him a few items he had already collected as evidence.

At last Inspector Sharma sighed tiredly, "These facts do make some sense to me, but they are not fully conclusive," he rubbed his temples with some anguish. "Now, if we can have some confessions, maybe....."

"I can arrange that for you, Inspector," said Ned zealously. "Just give me a few hours' time."

The D-Day

*T*he day of my wedding dawned on me all too soon. Sara was the one who stayed by my side and helped me get ready. She tried to maintain a happy façade for me but there were moments when the smile plastered on her lips slipped, giving way to a melancholy expression. I realized that she was feeling miserable.

It was then that it happened.

Sid was beside Sara out of nowhere. Looking at his fingers grazing her cheek, his hand resting possessively on her arm and his gaze touching her lips I knew Sid was up to his old games. My suspicions were confirmed when I saw the look in his eyes. A predator on the prowl.

We had not even been married for an hour, I thought disgustedly. It was not long before my pain gave way to anger. I closed my eyes and controlled my erratically beating heart. With my chin held high and resolve in my heart I immediately detached myself from the group of people I was standing with and stopped Sid's game by joining them where they sat.

Sara had given Sid wrong signals at the engagement party, so the fault was partly hers but she wasn't emotionally stable at the time, Sid should have realized. I fully blame Sid for what happened after that. He should have known better than to put fat in the fire.

It was all a Burlesque

Truth is a twinkling firefly. In the daylight it may not be able to attract attention to its presence but when the sun lies down to sleep, covered in the blanket of clouds, the firefly's radiance can't be hidden any longer. It dances behind the thick growth of trees; plays hide and seek in the wake of the misty nights, nonetheless flashing from afar.

On the Royal Hill the sun was now safely under the thick cloak of clouds and the firefly bopping around was finally visible to the onlookers. Ned had been searching for it all along. The police report was to be submitted in a day's time and Ned had to bring forth the person, hiding in plain sight, wearing a mask of deceit.

To further his purpose Ned called forth a meeting much like the one KD had arranged a fortnight ago with only one significant addition; the presence of Inspector Sharma. The officer had agreed to give Ned a chance to prove his theory and had accompanied Ned to the palace.

Once again the tea house was set for tea for all nine of them, the Mehtas and the Dullas. The vines covering the trellises over the tea house were now devoid of any greenery. Autumn had forced it to shed its leaves, leaving it brown and bare. The scent of flowers was not potent anymore and there was a definite chill in the air signalling the approach of winter. The family was seated around the table much like that afternoon, the Dullas on one side and the Mehtas on the other with Biji presiding over the table sitting between them. Inspector Sharma pulled a chair towards the back and settled there unobtrusively.

KD stood by his chair. He looked hard at Ned and then at the Inspector, his eyes silently admonishing Ned for the officer's presence. Yuvi was sitting on his left in an uptight pose, his face quite expressionless. Sid sat facing Ned directly. Snuggled between her sons was Tina, her composure ruffled. Monica and Vikram were next, Vikram's hand resting protectively on Monica's shoulder. The circle ended with Sara, her eyes red-rimmed.

Ned looked at each face in turn, all outwardly composed with well-bred masks for faces.

"Why were you here last night?" KD asked Ned. The gatekeeper had informed him of the same early in the morning.

Monica cut in before Ned could reply.

"Ned wasn't here yesterday."

"You weren't here to meet your dear sister, then?" KD's eyebrows rose suspiciously.

With both KD and Monica staring questioningly at him, Ned got up from his seat and sauntered purposefully to the other end of the table, opposite Biji. He cleared his throat and spoke with authority:

"I *was* here last night," he paused for effect. "I was here to find the truth behind Gulab's death and I *did* find all the answers."

Sid leaned forward eagerly.

"You know who killed Gulab?"

Ned nodded, looking at his audience. He could not complain of any lack of attention. Every eye was fixed upon him. In the stillness you could have heard a pin drop.

Eyebrows furrowed and lips puckered, he declared. "Yes."

Monica's tea spilled on the saucer. Tina sucked in a shallow breath.

"Who?" KD asked, his body shrinking back as if expecting a blow.

Ned copied his lopsided crooked smile and pronounced as cruelly as he could, "Let us proceed my way this time, step by step. The way *I* want the truth to unfold."

Ned dragged a chair directly opposite Biji at the head of the table, a little away from the rest and stood near it. Taping its arm, he started in a carefully modulated unemotional voice:

"As you all know by now, Sara is exonerated in Gulab's murder case. It has been proved by the statement given by the maid, Upma, that her ear-ring was dropped on the scene of crime in order to implicate her."

KD interrupted, shaking his head steadfastly.

"What about the other evidence? We can't negate all that."

"What if I say that all that was forged?" Ned suggested with a raised eyebrow.

KD shook his head disbelievingly.

"All the evidence cannot be counterfeit," he was adamant.

"Okay. Let me list the evidences against her," Ned said placating. "First, Sara was awake between 2:00am and 4:00 am, the probable time of murder. Second, her ear-ring was found near Gulab's body. Third, a red hair was found on Sid's conjugal bed. Fourth, the poison was found in her room. Fifth, she prepared Sid's ceremonial milk, which was drugged. Sixth, the poison was taken from her laboratory. Seventh, a lady in white was witnessed on Sid's balcony the night of the murder, believed to be Sara."

Ned paused for breath.

"Have I left out anything?"

KD shook his head.

"As far as the first evidence goes, I think we can safely say that not only Sara but some of the other members of the family were also awake between 2:00am and 4:00 am," he looked knowingly towards Tina.

Tina shuffled in her seat, uneasy. Ned proceeded:

"The second evidence against Sara has already been discredited," he met KD's challenging eyes heads on. "The earring was a subterfuge to lay the blame on her."

Monica chimed in, "True."

"Now let us investigate the very baffling third proof, that of the mysterious red hair on Sid's conjugal bed." He eyed Monica thoughtfully, "Are you sure it was red?"

"Of course," she provided blithely. "I am very observant, if I may say so myself. Am I not, Vikram?"

She looked appealingly at her chubby husband.

"You are very vigilant, darling," Munching on a muffin, Vikram nodded lovingly at her. "She is never one to imagine things. She is your sister, you should know that!" His voice held a trace of reproof for Ned.

"Okay," Ned agreed gallantly. "For the time being, let us move on to the evidence of the gardener. He saw a lady in white on Sid's balcony around 4:30 am. Am I right?" he asked of Sid.

"Yes."

"Is he positive that it was a female?"

"Absolutely."

He cleared his throat, and went on:

"There were only four ladies in Ratnagiri Palace that night. We can safely exclude Biji from being that lady but we do know for a fact that Sara, Monica and Mrs. Mehta were awake between 2:00 am and 4:00 am," he rubbed his stubbled chin in reflection. "So it is safe to reason that the lady on the balcony *was* one of them."

"The maid Upma," Tina was quick to point out.

"Wasn't that lady," Ned regarded her steadily.

"It can't be me! I wasn't there on the balcony that night!" Monica interrupted. "It's disgraceful, Ned. Standing up there and saying such things!"

Monica huffed angrily.

"A little patience, sister. And be kind enough not to interrupt," said Ned

Monica tossed her head angrily.

"I insist on making my protest. Don't use my name for your conjectures."

"Monica was sleeping in our room at that time. I will vouch for her." Vikram butted in, holding onto her hand protectively.

Monica gazed adoringly at her beloved husband and patted his hand covering her own. It was evident to all that the shrew was madly in love with the clumsy guy, though no one could decipher why.

"How can you be sure, Vikram? You were sleeping at the time, dead to the world, remember?" Ned raised an eyebrow, "Or weren't you?"

Vikram's eyes instantly caught his mother's, suspicion

lurking in his. He hoped against hope that his mother hadn't repeated to anyone what she had told him.

He stammered, "Of course…. I was sleeping. But…"

"As he says, he *was* sleeping." Monica pronounced confidently.

"If you can guarantee for Vikram, it means *you* were awake? You didn't go to bed after putting Jack back to sleep?"

"I didn't." Monica agreed steely eyed.

Ned flopped on his chair and folding his legs, asked curiously:

"I know you hated Gulab but I could never understand the reason behind such blatant ruthless loathing. She wasn't that bad, was she now?"

"She was a tasteless girl, weird and rural. Not fit to be a part of our family," Monica pronounced haughtily.

Ned's brows came together in thought.

"Is that enough to infuse such red hot rage in your heart for her?"

Monica looked away, her head held high.

"The real reason you hated her this much is something else. Isn't it?" he asked sceptically. "It's the same reason which made you lie just now."

"What lie?" Monica fumbled.

"You were fast asleep by the time Sara left for her room. Wasn't she?" Ned looked at Sara interrogatively.

Sara couldn't help but nod in assent.

"You are obsessively in love with your husband," Ned turned to Monica. "You are even ready to lie in order to protect him," Ned's pitch raised with each word. "The truth is - you didn't hate Gulab. You were jealous of her." Ned went to her. "Vikram was too fond of her for your liking, wasn't he?" Ned asked with compassion.

"Monica is never jealous!" Vikram intervened. "She is a cool and composed lady. Don't just say anything you want to!" He held onto her hand tightly. "And anyways, why should she be jealous of Gulab? Gulab was like my little sister."

Sara smiled painfully, "Love is unreasonable, senseless."

"No one except us siblings know what is really behind the cool façade our sister hides under. Monica is too passionate for her own good." He smiled at his elder sister and taking her hand in a soft grasp, kissed it lovingly. "Monica was never insecure about Gulab's political clout or money. She was just extremely jealous of the bond between Vikram and Gulab. This jealousy transcended into hate when Gulab helped Vikram and Monica couldn't."

Ned faced the occupants of the table once again and spoke with confidence.

"But Gulab was helping her husband materialize his lifelong dream, Monica knew that too well. So, maybe she resented her or hated her but she could never have killed her," he smiled at his sister. "My sister loves Vikram too much to let her own insecurities ruin his dreams."

Monica looked up at him, the colour slowly rising in her face at having her well guarded emotions flaunted so openly. "All you have said is quite true." She smiled shyly at Vikram's soft, "I love you, darling."

"But what about the sleeping pills hidden in her room?" Tina asked Ned.

"You searched my room!" Monica was aghast but still managed to look dignified. "All this murder business was giving me insomnia so I got the pills prescribed from the doctor. I have the receipt for the medicine dated after the murder, I can show you if you want. I didn't want to worry Vikram unnecessarily, so I hid them. My poor love was already quite upset."

Tina nodded with understanding. "I even took the saffron from Biji's room and got it tested from the lab."

"It was clean. Wasn't it?" Biji scoffed. "I am no fool."

Ned shook out of this emotional exchange and caught up from where he had been interrupted, "As I was saying, that lady on the balcony could have been anyone of these three women. Now that we have ruled out Monica only Mrs. Mehta and Sara could have been on the balcony." He looked hard first at Tina who was looking more flustered by every passing minute and then at the self-possessed Sara.

"Now I ask you all, won't it make sense if the lady on the balcony was the same person whose hair was on the pillow? The lady was in Sid's room, it can very well be her hair on the bed." He stressed, "The *red* hair."

Sid gave a quick nod of comprehension.

"I agree."

"Then it *was* Sara!" Vikram gasped.

Ned walked slowly towards the table and stopped where Tina was sitting, silently sipping her tea.

"What do you think, Mrs. Mehta? Was that lady Sara?"

"I don't know...ah," she faltered. Her hand holding the tea cup was shaking uncontrollably and Ned took the cup from her and placed it on the table.

All eyes on Tina, she stood up, trying to side step Ned to leave the table. Biji's officious, "Sit down!" stopped her attempts to run away and she settled uncomfortably on the edge of her seat.

"Tina was awake that night. We all know that," KD folded his arms over his chest. "But that doesn't prove that she was in Sid's room. Moreover she is a brunette; it can't be her hair on the bed. Do you need my glasses to see that?" KD removed his glasses and offered them to Ned insultingly.

"Sir, I think you need them more than I do for looking at this," Ned took out a picture from his pocket and presented it to KD with a flourish.

KD stared at it for a few seconds before looking at his wife in horror and then back at the picture.

"What is it, KD?" Biji asked.

Upon seeing his father dumbfounded and his mother unable to meet anyone's eyes, Yuvi, sitting next to him, peeked over KD's shoulder to look at the picture. He sucked in a quick breath. "Oh!"

"Pass it to me," Biji ordered.

KD handed over the picture to Yuvi who passed it around the table to finally reach Biji. It was a picture from Sid and Gulab's wedding album and Tina was sporting red bangs in the image.

"Had completely forgotten about Mom's hair style…" Yuvi looked at his mother rubbing her hands in agitation. "But now I do remember her telling me about going to the spa to get off the fiery red highlights she was sporting for the marriage….but Mom changes her hairdos every other week…we never seem to remember them," he thought aloud.

"What the hell!" Sid stood up angrily. "Have you anything to do with my wife's murder?" he asked his mother accusingly.

"Were you in Sid's room that night?" Biji's voice had

suppressed anger lining it.

Tina cringed under the attack but replied weakly with a shamefaced, "Yes." She was quick to add with a pleading expression, her gaze traversing over the unbelieving faces of her family.

"But I had nothing to do with Gulab's murder. I promise!" She beseeched in a pained voice, "Trust me."

"I don't trust you. Not at all. If you didn't have anything to hide, why didn't you come clean about this? Why?" Sid shouted angrily.

KD banged his palm on the table with force, shaking the fragile bone china cups, and spoke heatedly.

"Leave the woman alone!" His nostrils flared, "I expected more out of you, Sid. Where did the value of family solidarity I have been preaching about for years go, if not in your brain?"

He threw him a reproachful glance. Sid had the grace to look apologetic and Vikram's eyes lit up for a minute. Now Sid was getting what he deserved, he thought with a smirk.

Ned slipped in lithely, drawing all eyes back to him.

"Maybe Mr. and Mrs. KD Mehta are in it together. Humn?" He looked at KD with a gleam in his eyes. He moved slowly towards KD and holding the back of his chair added over his shoulder, "We all know you resented Gulab for helping out Vikram. You tried everything you could in the last three months to make her back out of the agreement. And see! Before she could sign on the dotted line, she is dead, and the Mehta family stays together. A happy ending!" He finished triumphantly, "God has his extreme blessings on you, Sir."

After a few seconds in which KD's eyes duelled with his, Ned added with insinuation clear in his voice:

"Or maybe the great Mr. KD Mehta lent a hand to God." he left the sentence unfinished.

KD smirked at him without replying.

"Nothing to say?" Ned prodded flippantly.

KD tilted his chair without warning, dislodging Ned's hands away from it. His crooked smile back in place, KD beamed mockingly. "Think whatever you like."

The silence that ensued was thick. Tina broke it with a muttered, "Trust me, I …we….didn't murder Gulab." She looked at her husband for support but none came.

"I know that you didn't kill Gulab," Ned took pity on her. He addressed the group:

"Mrs. Mehta *was* in Sid's room that nigh and it *was* her hair on the bed but she is no murderer."

"Then what was she doing in my room on my wedding night?" Sid asked impatiently.

Tina just looked down at her hands, wringing them agitatedly in her lap. KD could no longer restrain himself. He burst out passionately:

"Don't you know by now that your mother is a dipsomaniac? An alcoholic!" He breathed fire. "Why couldn't you add it up yourself, my intelligent son? Didn't you find a bottle of liquor taken from your recently stocked bar on our balcony?" He asked heatedly. "She was stealing alcohol from your room that night. What else?!"

There was a sudden outburst of sobs. Tina took out her handkerchief and cried into it.

"It's been dreadful," she sobbed.

Sid looked at Tina wonderingly, aghast. "I had no idea."

Tina stuttered, "It is true. At Sid's wedding, I couldn't publically consume much, so, after we came home, I couldn't control the urge any longer. I sat there on the balcony away from KD's scrutiny and closed the glass doors from inside. I kept the chair near the wall so that no one could see me from outside," she continued with a small sigh, "I finished the bottle of tequila in our room and decided to scout the bar downstairs for more. I was about to go down when I happened to see that the door to Sid's room was open. I peeked inside and found Sid deep in sleep and Gulab's side of the bed empty. I thought she was in the washroom and quickly came in to take a bottle from the mini bar before anyone could see me. I was inebriated and not very stable on my feet so while trying to get up after taking the bottle from the bar, I kind of fell on the bed, half on Sid. I think that is how my hair came to be on the pillow. I panicked and in my drunken state, rushed into the balcony to hide from Sid in case he got up. I waited there for a few minutes and when Sid didn't wake up and I tiptoed to my own room."

She bowed her head. "I...uh...didn't want anyone to find out about my addiction. If I had thought it would do the investigation any good by revealing these facts, I would have done so. But it didn't seem to me to bear upon the case."

Ned shot a quick glance at Tina. She was very pale but her emotions were under control now that she had the weight lifted off her chest.

"In a sense, that is correct, Mrs. Mehta. Though these details have cleared my mind of many misconceptions, and left me free to see other facts in their true significance," said Ned, smiling.

Ned resumed his lecturing manner. "Now that we have

eliminated most of the evidences against Sara, why don't we quit playing games and cut to the chase." He paced around the table and hovered behind Vikram, Yuvi and Sid.

Everyone held their breath.

"We can definitely ask our eye witnesses to put a spot light on our murderer."

There was a stir of excitement in the group upon hearing this.

"Eye witnesses," Yuvi exclaimed, astonished. "Impossible! There are no eye-witnesses."

"You are joking, Ned!" Monica expostulated.

"Who?" Vikram's round eyes were bulging out of their sockets with surprise.

"An eye witness!" KD cried.

"Not one, but two." Ned continued unheeded.

"Jack and Jill," He pronounced forcefully. "They didn't realize it and neither did we but the twins, in a way, did catch the murderer in the act."

"They saw Gulab being murdered?" Yuvi's eyes opened wide.

"When did they see it?"

"Why didn't they tell us?"

"Who murdered Gulab?"

"Call the twins, why don't you?"

Ned was bombarded with a flurry of questions from all directions. He held out his hand to signal them all to be quiet.

"You remember," he addressed them collectively again, "the twins playing 'ghost'?"

The assembled party nodded their assent and Ned continued, "Both Jack and Jill claim to have had nightmares the night

Gulab died. I know that they are not muddled in their belief, as children this young can be, because they woke up crying in fright. I questioned the children and their description of their dreams is exactly the same except that Jack is not really sure about the colour of the ghost's claws and Jill is.

"What I asked myself is – how can two children have exactly the same dream? And after much deliberation I concluded that they couldn't. But why would they lie, I asked myself repeatedly and was presented with only one answer," he paused. "They are not lying. They didn't dream a ghost but they actually saw one. I remembered Monica telling me quite often that the twins are very light sleepers," he looked towards Monica for confirmation and at her assent continued, "Now what if Jack actually heard someone moving around the room that night and in the darkness got scared and started crying. He related that scary feeling to a nightmare and the person in the room to be a part of his dream. This is what happened to Jill as well. The only difference being that when Jill had the 'nightmare', it was early morning and she could see the 'ghost' more clearly."

"Even if you are correct, it just means that someone came in Sara's room that night and early in the morning. That someone need not be Gulab's murderer," KD supplied.

"Anyway, who was he?" Sid asked interestedly, "Or she?"

"I have an answer to that as well. I asked the children a few questions and got some interesting answers. He was a 'man ghost', 'tall ghost', 'lean ghost'.

"I hope you all don't believe in ghosts?" Ned joked. "The ghost had a shawl draped around him so the children couldn't recognize him but he was actually a man, a man present in the palace that night. We have five options to choose from. Mr. KD Mehta, Sid, Vikram, Yuvi or me." He looked attentively at each man in turn and then continued, "Vikram is neither tall nor lean, so that keeps him out. The children don't think that the ghost wears glasses, so I assume that the ghost couldn't be Mr. KD Mehta who can't function without his glasses. Now, that leaves us with me, Sid and Yuvi.

"Sid had a lot to profit by Gulab's death."

Sid got up. His voice rang out, cold as steel, "I realize very well what you are suggesting. You are saying - are you not? - that I killed Gulab. You bastard!" Sid cried. "Don't you dare suggest that I killed my wife!"

"I wasn't suggesting anything of the kind. Mrs. Mehta has vouched for you just now. She fell heavily on you but you didn't wake up. It means that you were actually drugged and sleeping placidly around the time the murder was committed. This is what I meant when I said her statement cleared my misconceptions."

Placated, Sid sat down once again. Ned turned to Yuvi.

"That leaves us with only one person."

"Aren't you forgetting that even you are un-vouched for?" Yuvi met Ned heads on.

"Exactly," said KD dryly.

Slowly, Ned swung around. His eyes, hard and contemptuous, ranged over the faces turned towards him.

He said, "You blind fools - all of you. Don't you know that if I'd done it I would have confessed? I'd never have let Sara suffer for what I'd done. Never!"

"I agree," said Sid, following things out in his mind.

"Well, there is one more thing exonerating me," Ned said placidly, "the claws of the ghost."

"Claws? What claws?" KD asked Ned.

"The funnily wrapped hands are the ghost's claws. Jill is confident that they were made with crepe bandages just like the ones Biji wraps around her knees."

"What about these claws?" Yuvi asked nonchalantly.

"I didn't have any crepe bandage with me that night but you definitely had."

"Why would I be wrapping crepe bandage around my hands?"

"Well…they were your makeshift gloves, I believe."

"I don't even know where my crepe bandage is. I haven't had an accident in the past six months."

Tina sucked in a breath and looked at Sid askance. Their eyes met and both of them remembered their huddled conversation while checking out Vikram's dresser. Yuvi had hidden his crepe bandages in his underwear cabinet.

"Then why does Sara seem to think that you had an accident around Sid's wedding?" Ned asked. He turned to the quiet figure at his elbow.

Sara offered:

"I can swear that he had an accident around that time."

Yuvi asked Sara in a lazy drawl, "Did you hear me say that I had an accident?"

"No." Sara shook her head.

"Did you witness that accident?" Yuvi asked sceptically.

"No." Sara repeated perplexedly and slowly, "No, I, did not see it -" She paused, frowning. "And yet I know."

Yuvi raised his eyebrows questioningly and then shrugged as if resting his case.

Ned supplied unperturbed, "My dear friend, neither did

you recount a tale about your accident to Sara and nor did she witness it," he paused meaningfully, "but she does remember the crepe bandage tied on your arm the day the police was here for the interrogation. And that is why Sara assumed you had an accident."

Sara said wonderingly, "That makes perfect sense! Of course I remember now. The crepe bandage on his arm made me assume about the accident. I saw it."

Monica joined in, "So did I."

Ned turned to Yuvi.

"I think, you firstly used the crepe bandage as a makeshift glove and then surreptitiously tied it on your arm so that the police don't find it in your room as it may have had traces of poison on it," he paused. "You fit the description of the ghost. You are tall, slender, and had crepe bandage handy. By the process of elimination, it is safe to say that it was you who was in Sara's room that night."

Yuvi didn't deny the allegation this time.

"How does it matter?" Yuvi asked impatiently. "It has nothing to do with Gulab's murder."

"You are correct," Ned agreed. "This has nothing to do with Gulab's murder." He added angrily, "But you never wanted to murder Gulab. Your target was someone else, wasn't it?"

"What do you mean?" Vikram cried.

Ned looked Yuvi in the eye and declared:

"'I conjectured, and conjectured rightly that Yuvi's target was not Gulab," he paused for effect. "It was Sara."

"What?!" The cry of surprise was universal. Even Inspector Sharma pitched in.

Yuvi sat back in his chair unperturbed and looked around

him in silence.

"I remembered the look on Yuvi's face during the engagement party while he was escorting Gulab down. His eyes were filled with admiration and love for his best friend. He had been so protective of her when Sara created that ugly scene. I remembered the abhorrence on his face for Sara as well. And as soon as I remembered that look, the jigsaw of Gulab's death fitted perfectly for me.

"Yuvi went into Sara's room that night to find something of hers to drop near Gulab's body so that he could implicate her."

"That was Yuvi?" Tina interrupted. She looked at Vikram apologetically. "In my drunken haze I...I...uh...thought it was Vikram."

Ned continued as if she hadn't spoken.

"Jack saw him cloaked in a shawl, couldn't recognize him and started crying. He rushed out and waited in his room for the coast to clear. In the early morning, he tried his luck again, and this time carried out both of his tasks successfully, though Jill did see him as he was leaving the room. He stole Sara's ear-ring and before the body could be detected, dropped it near Gulab's body. He also planted traces of poison in Sara's room which he picked up from the pavilion lying near Gulab's body. And this was the reason for the otherwise late riser Yuvraj waking up before anyone else that morning," Ned smiled. "But what he hadn't bargained for was the maid trying on Sara's jewels in the night and hence giving her an alibi."

Again Yuvi did not deny the allegations.

Sid rushed towards him in anger. "What the fuck! You were Gulab's best friend. How could you kill her?"

Before Sid could deal him a blow Ned intervened:

"Yuvi could never harm a hair on Gulab's head, let alone murder her."

"He didn't?" Sid's hand stopped just in time before connecting with Yuvi's chest. He looked at Ned, confused.

"No," Ned offered. "Yuvi just wanted to frame Sara."

"Why?"

"Only Yuvi can shed light on his thoughts, but I think he somehow blamed Sara for Gulab's death. And believing in the maxim 'an eye for an eye' wanted her to hang and die for killing his dearest friend. In short, he wanted to murder Sara by incriminating her as Gulab's murderer."

Yuvi was still silent.

"Sara killed Gulab?" Sid asked forehead furrowed in thought.

Ned shook his head. "No. But someone who had the opportunity to drug your milk as well as take the poison from Sara's lab did."

"But....but only Sara could have done that!"

Ned shook his head. "No," he said quietly. "There was someone else as well who had access to both the milk and the poison," Ned looked round the room, and then pronounced impressively, "Gulab herself!"

Everyone looked at him, aghast.

"Yes. Gulab wasn't murdered. She committed suicide," he finished sadly.

Vikram rose to his feet. Sara gave a little gasp.

"Suicide?" A horrified incredulous sigh from Tina.

A stare, a very blank stare from Yuvi.

A sharp incisive "Suicide?" from Monica.

A "Good God!" from Biji.

"Impossible!" Sid exclaimed. "We just got married!"

"My thoughts, exactly," thought Inspector Sharma.

"Nevertheless, my friend, it was Gulab. Because, in no other way can you account for the facts of the drugged milk and the stolen poison otherwise. Gulab had the perfect opportunity to drug your milk after Sara handed it to her and she had been to Sara's lab as well the day she cut her foot on the glass."

Sara gasped. "Are you insane, Ned? Why would she?"

"Why would she?" Vikram repeated askance.

"Looking at the matter psychologically, I drew one conclusion which I am convinced is correct." He paused, "The key to understanding Gulab's motive is hidden in the story of her life. Let us reconstruct it.

"A child of a broken marriage, unappreciated by her family, she finds refuge with Sid. The Mehtas accept her into their stronghold and the shy girl blossoms in their midst. She strongly believes herself to be a part of this family, her future secure with Sid. She turns a blind eye to Sid's many faults, his flirtatious nature and even his infidelities. But one day, her safe haven is pulled from under her when she witnesses Sid professing his love for Sara. Gulab had never made any backup plan for her life so when her life crumbles, she is at sea, not knowing how to live anymore. Had she been a normal girl with support of parents or friends, she would have coped like the other heartbroken girls. But with Sid gone, she lost her friends, family and supporters as well. She was orphaned once again.

"This was when I entered her life. I saw her for what she was, an extremely sensitive and loving girl seeking desperately to belong. She was a beautiful human being and I couldn't help but fall in love with her. Her goodness even wooed my sister who had all the reasons to be wary of her. At last Gulab became a part of our small happy family. She was extremely fond of Sara and me. She was ready to marry me, but before she could do that, Sid re-entered her life. He wanted to possess the new improved Gulab and in the process humiliated his fiancée, Sara. Gulab was the kind of girl who could do anything for her family, for her loved ones. She was extremely loyal and what Sid had forgotten was that now we were her family. The Mehtas were outsiders, even if she loved Sid.

"What happened next is mere guesswork on my part, but I should say that she agreed to marry Sid to get Sara away from his clutches. She wanted Sara to have a happy life which she was sure the unfaithful Sid could never offer her. But at the engagement ceremony and on her wedding day, she saw Sid trying to woo Sara once again. Gulab didn't appreciate it and finally her pent up anger exploded. It was then that she planned on taking revenge on Sid."

"What a fantastic story!" KD sneered. "She would take revenge from Sid by killing herself? You expect us to believe this?"

"If she did commit suicide for this reason, I can safely say that the girl was a nutcase. Good riddance!" Biji derided bitingly.

"This entire hullabaloo about a murder for nothing!" Monica sighed. "The girl was screwed up!"

Suddenly, with electrifying effect, Yuvi burst into speech.

"Shut up all of you! Shut up! Gulab was perfectly sane. The poor girl suffered terribly for *your* sister," he eyed Monica with distaste, "*Your fucking sister!* My Gulab was ready to give away her life to a cheater because she wanted to protect your sister.

Sara deserved that painful death, not my darling friend. Not Gulab." His blood red eyes shot daggers at Monica. "The gall to call *my Gulab* insane!"

Monica snorted ever so slightly. She met the animosity in his eyes with a complete lack of interest.

Ned did not allow himself to be angered by his sister's vile remarks. He said:

"Yuvi, these people should know what happened that night, otherwise they will never respect Gulab as she deserves. People like Monica will always call her crazy."

"Please!" he pleaded. "Tell them everything."

Yuvi looked around the table, at the pleading expression of Ned, the red rimmed eyes of Sara, and his face filled with misery. An inner battle ensued and he came to a decision. He murmured distractedly, remembering that awful night, "I couldn't sleep that night because my AC had broken down. I went out to the balcony for some fresh air. I saw Gulab on the Pavilion, she was dancing. I couldn't see Sid with her, so I decided to go check on her. When I reached her, I called out, but she was deaf to my voice. I didn't know that something was wrong with her at the time. I didn't disturb her, just stood there looking at her. After a few minutes, she glided to the floor, tired but smiling. I decided not to disturb her and was going back to my room when I heard a strange sound. I could immediately see that she was having trouble breathing. By the time I reached her, there was nothing I could do. She was gone. There were some capsules lying near her. I deduced that they were poisonous. I had touched them, my fingerprints were on them, so I emptied their contents on a paper, folded it and placed it in Sara's bedroom. To incriminate her, I also stole her ear-ring and dropped it near Gulab just like Ned said," there was rage in his eyes. "Sara deserved to die, not my Gulab. Not her!"

He broke down.

"But this – this doesn't mean Gulab committed suicide," Sid spoke slowly.

Sara objected. "Why didn't she leave a suicide note?"

Ned interrupted her in a flash: "Yes, why? Why did Gulab try so desperately to establish that she didn't commit suicide. No trace of poison on her, no last note for her loved ones?"

He paused, a long pause in which he looked unblinkingly at Yuvi. They were like duellists on guard. There was a momentary silence fraught with tension but at last Ned broke it with a decree:

"Gulab did leave behind a note."

"I threw it away," said Yuvi, an aggressive note in his voice.

"No, you didn't."

Ned went on quickly, ignoring the gathering storm visible on Yuvi's face.

"Dear All," said Ned, with a flourish, "the last link of the chain is now in my hands. Let me show you the suicide note."

Amid breathless excitement, he held out a sheet of paper.

There was shocked distaste on Yuvi's face. A howl that was almost a scream broke the silence. "You devil! How did you get it?" Yuvi shouted.

A chair was overturned. Ned skipped nimbly aside. A quick movement on his part, and his assailant fell with a crash but not before snatching at the page in Ned's hand.

Sid and Vikram held onto a struggling Yuvi, his arms thrashing wildly. Inspector Sharma joined them with haste. "I would advise you to co-operate Mr. Yuvraj Mehta, or I'll arrest you for obstruction of justice," he threatened with force but Yuvi just kept on struggling mindlessly.

At Ned's "Gulab meant it to be found, Yuvi. It was her last wish. *Your Gulab's last wish,*" Yuvraj caved in and huffing loudly, hunkered down on the grass, broken.

Ned continued, "I found it out by a chance remark of Gulab's about Yuvi keeping her trinkets as a lucky charm in his Harley windshield bag. Knowing Gulab, I was sure that she would leave behind a last note. I knew Yuvi could never destroy her last memory. I proceeded to reason on that assumption and searched the bag and as expected, found Gulab's letter hidden there. It was the perfect place to hide it as no one was interested in its contents and chances of its discovery were minimal." He looked at Yuvi, "I am sorry I had to break the lock."

"There were a few capsules filled with the poison and a vial along with this letter. I disposed of them before anyone could discover the body," Yuvi supplied.

"Why didn't you want to show it to us?" Sid asked Yuvi, baffled. "I am grieving for her, it could have helped me," he huffed angrily.

"Grieving for her?" Yuvi scoffed. "Don't think I don't know about your debts and your only grief being to clear it as soon as you can lay hands on Gulab's money!"

"She was my wife. I had a right to her last letter!" Sid shouted with anger. "Wasn't it my right irrespective of my debts?"

Yuvi stoically remained silent and turned his face away, hiding the tears welling in his eyes from gathering. "I hate you, Sid! I hate you," he mouthed silently.

In the deathly silence, Ned unruffled the papers. There was a formal suicide note for the police and a letter for Sid. He passed on the note to the Inspector and clearing his throat, he read the letter:

Sid,

In the book of life, every page has two sides. We human beings fill one with our plans, hopes and wishes and destiny writes on the other side. Sid, it has never been our fate to be together. There's just no way forward for us in this life.

If you prick me, do I not bleed? If you tickle me, do I not laugh? If you poison me, do I not die? And if you wrong me, shall I not take revenge?

Sara and Ned are my family now, and I can't sit back while you hurt them. There are no apologies for some mistakes, just punishments. And yours is to love someone when there is no chance of that love ever thriving. Isn't it what you made me, Sara and a lot many other trusting hearts go through?

I think it's time I let you go. This is hard to do because a part of me is still in love with you, but I don't have any other option.

Had I died in any other situation, I would have asked you to forget me and move forward in your life. But I can't afford that courtesy for you. For you I have only one message:

'Forget-me-not' and to remind you of this every day of your life, I am leaving behind with this letter a crystal posy of beautiful blue forget-me-nots, just like the ones you used to send me.

Gulab

PS – I know Vikram didn't get the partnership deeds signed on the allotted day because he was in talks with a few friends to take my place. He wanted to oust me from the business. Attached with this letter is a bank account with Vikram as the beneficiary after my demise. Tell him that it was never my intention to rule over him, I was just trying to help him out. I would like him to use these funds and catch his dreams. At least someone should.

Gulab's scribbled words in Ned's heavy voice were greeted with a stunned silence. Sara put her hand to her mouth to stifle a cry, her eyes moist, then slowly moved back to the chair and sat, staring at the floor. Vikram lowered his head and leaned on his wife for support. Ned handed down the bank details to Vikram.

There was a long silence.

Inspector Sharma folded the suicide note and placed it in his front pocket. "I'll come for a detailed statement tomorrow," he said and discreetly left the party alone.

"You don't have to worry about your debt, Sid," Vikram approached him quietly. "We will handle it together. Gulab has been too generous with me," he looked at the bank details. "We will repay every single penny you owe."

Sid didn't pay any heed to him. His face had gone rather white. He rose; an incredulous look on his face. He stepped towards Ned, half raising his arm, unable to grasp the full meaning of Gulab's words. "She…" he murmured. "She…"

Ned said gently:

"Was it not the best way to punish you? She thought so."

Sid buried his face in his hands. Ned came forward and laid a hand on his shoulder.

In a broken voice Sid said, "I understand love now. Ever since Gulab died, I have had this regret punching me every few minutes that what I did to her was wrong. She had loved me wholeheartedly and I cheated on her. Even after our wedding, I entertained thoughts of wooing Sara back. I abused her trust, her love. I deserve this loneliness. I deserve this punishment."

Sid said wistfully:

"She was much too good for me, always."

In the silence that followed - a horrified, appalled silence - everyone left the table one by one.

The sky was now growing dark, the last rays of the sun throwing shadows on the stone walls of the Palace. Sid was alone in the garden, his face strewn with tears and his thoughts his only companions. After Gulab's death, he had started missing her so much that he wanted to rip her out of his dreams and bound her to him so that they were always together. He had never felt like this for anyone in his life. Gulab's death had opened a flood gate of unknown and unconceivable emotions inside him. Now they had splurged in full fury and carried away effortlessly on their high tides, the man he had once been. The soul left behind was someone he barely recognized, someone who looked like him, talked like him but who didn't feel like him. This new man finally realized what love was. He was entrapped in its cobwebs but instead of shrugging them off with a swift jerk, he moved with deliberate ease so as not to tear the fragile threads surrounding him with tenderness.

"I have no will to weep or sing,

No least desire to pray or curse;

The loss of love is a terrible thing;

They lie who say that death is worse."

In a hauntingly sad voice, the connoisseur of poems, quoted from 'The Loss of Love' by Countee Cullen, in true love at last.

A Victim of Love

*D*id it surprise you to find that I am not who you thought I was? That I'm not exactly how I played myself out to be?

I told you that I had hidden something in my pocket while leaving Sara's laboratory. Did you never pause to consider what it could have been and why was I sharing that fact with you?

You should have. It was an early confession from my side; the confession to killing Gulab Sarin and becoming Rose forever.

Love came knocking on my door thrice, though I didn't realize it at the time; I was lost in a blaze of my own. The first knock was cloaked in the attire of friendship. It paraded before my eyes for years but just like we can't read a book if held too close to our eyes, I wasn't able to understand the feelings of this person whom I held much too close to my heart. The second knock was the romantic interlude of my life to which I surrendered passionately. My days and nights filled with longing for my sweetheart was the sweetest agony of love I was fortunate enough to experience. The third knock was a feather light caress of affection which touched my heart with its selflessness. My withered heart burgeoned with its touch.

For Yuvraj, the strong bond of fondness between us was the mother of this emotion. I started out as his best friend, over time *he understood me and admiration seeped in and when I went to Mumbai he missed me tremendously and suddenly stronger emotions took hold of his heart. But as destiny would have it, he was never able to express his love for me.*

Until it was too late.

His love spilled from his eyes and lips for the girl dressed as a bride, convulsing violently in his arms. It spilled for the girl who was professing her love for another man, bidding him to be her messenger. It spilled for the girl, without any coercion, who was about to leave him forever. The weight of this pain unhinged him with rage. After reading my letter he had stuck to the belief that had Sara not entered our lives I would still be alive and he planned to make her pay for taking me away from him.

The second knock was Sid. He was like a butterfly, which sits on every flower, but belongs to none. He thrived on the novelty of a passionate frenzy never wanting it to subside, not wanting to accept that enduring love is much more than the excitement of a first glance, first kiss or the burning desire for someone. He moved from one partner to another falling in and out of love as quickly as the changing seasons.

Sid had toyed with my feeling for years but I still couldn't let go of my love for him. I had forgiven him though, leaving my dark past where it belonged and was ready to welcome a new dawn into my life. But he wouldn't let me be. He discredited both our feelings, Sara's and mine. Sara's unhappiness would have affected not only her but Ned as well, who felt her pain more potently than his own. I didn't have an option but to save them both. Had I not married Sid, Sara would never have backed away from marrying him, so lost in his charm was she. The only way to save her was to accept Sid's proposal. I won't lie though; the idea wasn't repulsive to me. Sid is my favourite mistake.

But things didn't progress as planned. On the day of our wedding Sid was ready to despoil what was no longer his own and in the process destroy the serenity of another loving heart. I saw red. To my fuming mind he seemed like a pillager who had decided that he had exploited his first prey enough and was now ready to plunder a greener pasture. The fact that he'd already ransacked me and Sara a number of times in the past and with much effort we'd prospered once again didn't draw his pity let alone his consideration. My blood boiled for revenge, not only for myself and Sara but for those other trusting hearts as well who he had trampled on.

It was time for Sid to taste his own medicine, I vowed. Sid needed to welter in the bitter agony of unrequited love, just like me, I decided there and then. I became so truculent in my vengeance that I didn't shy away from becoming a murderess. I murdered myself. Happily.

Sitting with Sid after our wedding, hiding behind a façade of smile, I'd silently planned and plotted to end my life.

I'd read a quote by Lord Byron, long ago when I was just a girl and now resolved to follow it to the end.

"Think you, if Laura had been Petrarch's wife, He would have written sonnets all his life?"

The thirsty will run after water till the time his thirst is not quenched, I reasoned. So, I decided to leave Sid in the throes of unquenched passion, never letting him appease it. The butterfly was left hankering for the flower he could never have and to him it became the most appealing of all. It was his sentence to grovel for release from this unbearable pain. He would beg to be free of it but love is merciless, once stricken with it no medicine can cure you of its effects. I remembered the day when I was listening in on Sara and Ned's conversation in her lab and had wanted to die after witnessing the bitterness in their hearts for me. In my frantic state

I had seen the bottle of cyanide neatly labelled in the cupboard I was hiding behind and had kept it in my pocket to swallow it and end my life. But as destiny would have it, I dropped a bottle while reaching for the cyanide and cut my foot on it and I witnessed Ned's true feeling for me and forgot about killing myself, finally at peace. That vial was still with me and I decided to use that poison now. I filled it into capsules and kept it in my bag, the plan already concreted in my head.

I'm sorry for dying the way I did but not for what I did to Sid's heart. He deserved it.

The only reason I am sorry for dying is Ned. Ned was a stranger I had accidently encountered in a very susceptible phase of my life. He showed me the fragrance of love and happiness without expecting anything in return. He just loved the loveless pulp that was left of me, the nectar already disposed off. He taught me that selflessness is the greatest expression of love.

Maybe subconsciously I was in love with him for a long long time, but I only realized the potency of my feelings for him when I stepped over the brink and was falling in a deep gorge knowing full well that I could never survive this fall.

I recognized my true love only as I lay dying. Swallowing the poison, I closed my eyes peacefully. There was only one image that flashed before me. The image of a man engulfed in the fumes of cigarette holding out the key to my happiness, finding his happiness in my smile. As the realization hit me, I couldn't stop myself from being elated. My last day became the happiest day of my life. I wanted to shout out to the world that I had finally found true love. My feet didn't hold still. In my happiness I danced. I danced till I couldn't anymore.

So, lying on my back, gazing fondly at the twinkling stars crooning softly to me from their perch on the beds of clouds, I thought about Ned. Taking a deep breath I closed my eyes capturing the vision of the effervescent night before it hid behind the twilight's curtain which I knew would soon be drawn. I knew I couldn't tell him how much I loved him, I didn't have enough time. The capsule I had swallowed had dissolved by then and I could feel the poison affecting my body. My eyes fell on Yuvi walking away from me and I saw a way. I didn't have enough energy to shout out to him. In the broken voice I could manage, I squeaked out his name and in the deadly stillness of the silent night, my plea reached his ears.

He turned instantly, a frown etched on his brow. It wasn't long before he guessed that everything was not alright with me, my body was twisting in spasms. He took my convulsing body in his arms and muttered in my ear about calling a doctor but I shook my head agitatedly and held onto his hand in as tight a grip I could manage. Torn by his desire to call a doctor and my wish to stay with him his eyes filled with helpless tears, he conceded, crooning softly his love for me. I managed to gather all my strength and pulling at the pendant around my neck feebly, looked suggestively at Yuvi. The years of silent understanding aided us and in no time he un-clutched my pendant from around my neck and laid it over my open palm. I mumbled very slowly the few words I could manage.

"For....Ned," I offered the pendant back to him, "Tell... him...I....love...him," I whispered.

My eyes were fluttering profusely as I willed myself to keep unconsciousness at bay but as soon as I managed to get my last words out I was at peace. I closed my eyes. I could hear Yuvi ruffling the letter I had left for Sid followed by his cries of protest. He held me close to his chest, hugging me tight as if he would not let me go, ever. He was repeating over and over how much he loved me and I was essentially happy to have him with me in my final seconds.

So, this is what happened to me, Gulab Sarin, the resident

weird girl of Ratnagiri.

Who would have guessed that what I couldn't get while I was alive would come to me after death.

Wasn't love all that I ever wanted?

Epilogue

Ned was standing on the Pavilion, clutching the balustrade. He felt the silent wind slowly passing by. With the sun about to go off to rest for the night, the cold evening breeze caressed his skin, ruffling his white shirt. A frown etching his forehead, Ned was breathing deeply, trying to get a whiff of Rose's special perfume. He had been looking out for some tell tale signs of Rose's presence for hours. But today the waters of the lake were motionless with no sudden ripples or an undulating shadow on its calm surface. The blades of grass in the garden did not bend to the invisible feet having stepped on them.

Ned was alone today with Rose gone forever.

The wind was in his hair, and Ned impatiently brushed it away from his forehead.

"Where are you?" There was desperation in his voice as he looked around him for her beloved silhouette.

A soft mellow voice answered, "Here she is."

Ned turned towards the bearer of that rich decree and stood staring at Yuvi, his palm open offering him Gulab's Silver Star hanging on its thin oxidized chain.

"She left this for you. I have been carrying it on me everywhere since her death," he smiled a sad lonely smile. "She wanted me to tell you that she loves you. It was her last wish."

Ned's heart clenched and he strained to control his tumultuous emotions. He closed his eyes and inhaled deeply. After a minute long silence, fraught with memories of his beloved, Ned opened his glistening eyes to look at the gift Rose had been telling him about in his dreams. She had left her most beloved possession for him and had even acquiesced to love him, Ned, and not Sid. She had left her money for Sid but her heart for him. His heart swelled with pleasure.

His pulse beating an erratic tune and hands shaking, he reached out to touch the locket. The pendant had been such an intricate part of her that he felt as if he was touching Rose herself. This realization broke the damn of self imposed restraint he had laid on himself and unbidden his glistening eyes crowded with salty tears. He glanced at Yuvi, his expression conveying his gratefulness to him.

"Thank you, my friend," he broke down and hugged him close. "Thank you."

Yuvi's defences that protected him from flaunting his feelings gave way when he encountered a love akin to the kind he himself felt. Both men vented their pain in that moment. After a while they sat companionably on the cold floor of the pavilion in silent understanding.

"Should have conveyed Gulab's message long ago," Yuvi spoke at last, reminiscently. "My sanity was feeding on revenge. It clouded my judgment. Can see now that Sara was not to blame for what happened to Gulab," he conceded albeit grudgingly.

After a long pause, he spoke feverishly:

"You know, I had wanted Gulab's star for myself. I didn't

want you to have it," he confessed. "I am jealous of you, Ned." He looked hard at him. "Why did she love you and not me?" There was pain in his eyes.

Ned didn't speak, just looked at Yuvi with compassion. "She loved you, Yuvi. As a friend. Her best buddy." Ned touched his shoulder sympathetically.

"Why did she have to die?" Yuvi spoke brokenly. "She took her last breaths in my arms, here, on this Pavilion," he looked around him shuddering with distaste. "I still don't understand how she could resort to suicide just for the sake of taking revenge on Sid?"

"Someone has rightly said that in love and revenge a woman is more barbaric than a man can ever be." Ned shrugged. "Moreover we should realize that Gulab was not a normal happy girl. She was already scarred by so many disappointments, her unloving family, infidelity and loneliness. All she had been left with was hope, hope for a better future. But when even that was snatched from her she didn't think she had much to live for. I can understand how revenge would have seemed like the best way out to her."

"She did wrong," Yuvi maintained.

"We all know that we have to make the right decisions in life. The problem is that we can't tell the difference between right and wrong. It is all a perspective," Ned smiled, a very tired smile.

In the silence that followed the sunset slowly flickered away, the last gleam leaving the pavilion where it had rested on the dark head and pale face of the girl dressed in her bridal finery standing there listening in on the conversation of the two men who had professed to love her. She walked away and from afar saw the night falling in on them. Yet, she was positive that they would recognize the fact that the golden glow of the day's sun comes not before the dark of night after but only after it. Their dark night would end soon she knew it in her heart. She turned to look back at them for a moment, a smile floating on her full lips, and then left them there, forever, reminiscing about the girl she had once been. Her beautiful red and golden dress with a matching net *dupatta* slowly dwindled into oblivion and the girl became a silhouette and then a shadow before finally becoming one with the dark night sky lit with millions of twinkling stars.